DISTURBI

Randal Mercier had made no secret of the fact that he had wanted Laura Hallam from the first moment he saw her—and Randal Mercier usually got what he wanted. But Laura loved Tom Nicol, had always loved him and always would. Then she learned that her father was in serious trouble, and the only way she could rescue him from it was to marry Randal ...

Books you will enjoy
by CHARLOTTE LAMB

AUTUMN CONQUEST

Two years ago Sara had realised that she could no longer bear to live with her husband Luke, and had left him. They had not met since—but now Luke had turned up again, apparently ready to discuss divorce. It meant that both he and she would now be free to marry again—so why wasn't Sara more delighted at the prospect?

DESERT BARBARIAN

When Marie Brinton remarked that she would be interested to learn more about the Arab way of life, she had hardly expected a handsome Arab to appear and sweep her off into the desert—but that was what happened. But the Arab was not what he seemed, and his influence on Marie's life was going to be very different from what she had imagined ...

MASTER OF COMUS

For the sake of her family's fortunes Leonie had agreed to an arranged marriage with her cousin Paul—whom she had always hero-worshipped anyway. But Paul had never been a one-woman man—and nothing about his behaviour suggested that marriage had changed him ...

CALL BACK YESTERDAY

When they were young Oriel Mellstock and Devil Haggard had been widely in love—but everything had gone wrong, and they had parted in bitterness and misunderstanding. Now Oriel was back, in the Yorkshire Dale where Devil still lived—but now could she put the clock back? For although she was free now, Devil was married ...

DISTURBING STRANGER

BY
CHARLOTTE LAMB

MILLS & BOON LIMITED
17-19 FOLEY STREET
LONDON W1A 1DR

All the characters in this book have no existence outside the imagination of the Author, and have no relation whatsoever to anyone bearing the same name or names. They are not even distantly inspired by any individual known or unknown to the Author, and all the incidents are pure invention. The text of this publication or any part thereof may not be reproduced or transmitted in any form or by any means, electronic or mechanical, including photocopying, recording, storage in an information retrieval system, or otherwise, without the written permission of the publisher.

First published 1978
Australian copyright 1978
Philippine copyright 1978
This edition 1978

© Charlotte Lamb 1978

For copyright reasons, this book may not be issued on loan or otherwise except in its original soft cover.

ISBN 0 263 72791 2

Set in Linotype Times 10 on 12pt

Made and printed in Great Britain by
Richard Clay (The Chaucer Press), Ltd., Bungay, Suffolk

CHAPTER ONE

THE wind blew fiercely along the river Thames, twisting the grey surface into a hundred broken ripples, setting moored barges rocking to and fro so that their warped timbers creaked, whipping through the branches of slender plane trees, eating into the bones of old men who slept out in secret corners of the night-time city, their huddled bodies under rustling piles of old newspapers. Pub signs swung on rusty hinges. Shutters clacked on shop windows. Dried leaves blew into drifts in empty doorways and made a rustling sea along the deserted city alleyways.

'London can be quite eerie at night,' said Laura Hallam, staring around her.

'It was your idea to come with me on this visit,' Pat Basset reminded her. 'I told you you'd find this district a bit alarming.'

'I'm glad I did,' Laura said soberly. 'Those poor children! It must be bad enough to lose your mother, but to have your father sent to prison on top of that must have been traumatic.'

'It happens every day,' Pat shrugged. 'We do the best we can. It isn't much. The kids you saw tonight are lucky. They have an aunt who's ready to take them in—there are a lot of others who have to be farmed out to strangers. That's much worse. I'm quite hopeful about the family we've just seen. They have a strong family tie, and that's half the battle.'

Laura had the distinct impression that Pat disapproved of her, and she wondered why. Was it because she was not one of the unlucky ones whom Pat cared for in her job as a social worker? Or because she had wanted to come tonight out of what Pat clearly regarded as vulgar curiosity? She did not want to explain to Pat that her motives were far more personal. Pat knew and worked with Tom. That was how they had met in the first place. Laura could never confide in someone who knew him.

They walked in silence for a while, their footsteps echoing down the narrow street. A door opened on the other side of the road and yellow light spilled out across the pavement. The silence was broken by laughter and loud voices. A young man came out, climbed on to a motor bike, kicked it once or twice and the engine sprang into roaring life. He disappeared down the street with a throb of departing sound.

Afterwards the silence seemed deeper. Passing a shabby shop Laura saw a man lounging in the doorway, and her nerves jumped at the hard stare he gave them. Pat ignored him. Laura was forced to marvel at her courage. Night after night she visited this run-down area of the city, walking the streets alone on most occasions. Once or twice, Laura knew, Pat had been attacked, even injured. Yet she had not given up her job. She was dedicated to the work she did.

Tom admired her, of course. She was the sort of woman Tom respected—brave, independent, caring. She lived in a tiny flat in a tenement, right in the heart of her district, and she devoted her whole life to her work.

As they passed under a street lamp Laura glanced sideways at her. Short, stocky, sallow-skinned, Pat had a customary frown on her square face, as though still pondering the problems she had just been dealing with, and her brown hair was ruffled by the wind into a tangled mass.

Abruptly she said now, 'Did Tom ask you to come with me tonight?'

Laura hesitated before replying. 'No,' she said after a long moment. 'It was entirely my own idea.'

'What did you expect to get out of it?' Pat demanded. 'A glimpse of how the other half lives?'

'A glimpse of Tom's world,' Laura said voluntarily, then felt herself flush, realising she had betrayed something she had not wished to let Pat guess.

Pat's frown deepened. 'Are you in love with Tom?' The question was harshly uttered.

Laura bit her lip before replying. 'That's a rather personal question,' she said lightly, trying to laugh. 'I'm not sure I want to answer it.'

'You just have,' Pat said in flat tones. 'I've been at this job long enough to know no one ever takes advice, but I've got to tell you that you're wasting your time. Tom isn't the man for you. The two of you are chalk and cheese.'

'You barely know me,' Laura said, wounded to the quick, any idea of denying Pat's suspicions completely forgotten.

'I know Tom,' Pat said simply.

A dark figure emerged from the shadows ahead of them, his footsteps ringing on the pavement with a regular sound. Laura jumped in surprise, her nerves tightening as they came nearer to him. Pat was unconcerned. Laura was surprised to see her smile and call out, 'Good evening. Cold night, isn't it?'

Then Laura saw why as the approaching figure moved into a yellow circle of lamplight and revealed himself as a uniformed policeman. He grinned at them.

'Bitter weather,' he agreed. 'On your rounds, Miss Basset? You've got a nice night for it. Seen Joey Prentice yet? His mum is dead worried about him. Seems he's been bunking out of school again. Since his dad ran off she hasn't been able to do anything with him. I said I'd mention it if I ran into you.'

'I'll call round tomorrow,' Pat sighed.

'A dog's life, isn't it?' The policeman grinned again, gave Laura a quick, curious look, his eyes widening as he took in her appearance. 'Evening, miss. You training alongside Miss Basset, are you?'

'No,' said Pat flatly. 'Just slumming.'

Laura flushed, hearing now the contempt openly expressed in the gruff voice. Obviously Pat was angry because Laura had asked if she might accompany her one night. It had not occurred to Laura that Pat might object. She had forgotten everything in her desire to snatch a glimpse of the world in which Tom Nicol worked.

The policeman took it for a joke and laughed as he said goodnight and walked on past them. Pat looked sideways at Laura, who saw that the cutting remark had been made deliberately. Pat had wished her to know how she felt.

As they crossed another of the dark, deserted roads a car screeched round the corner with a sound of scorching tyres and shot passed them, only to brake violently a moment later. Laura stopped dead, nervous once more, and looked at Pat to see how she took this new arrival.

Pat was staring at the car with a frown, which was not surprising since the car was very obviously out of place here—a long, sleek white sports car was hardly likely to belong to any of the tenants of the ramshackle little houses they had passed.

There were four occupants, all male. One by one they climbed out and confronted the two girls, laughing in a manner which convinced Laura that they were all drunk.

Their clothes matched the car—expensive, elegant, well-tailored clothes which had an odd air of dishevelment, as though the wearers had been to a wild party.

'What do you want?' Pat asked coldly, facing them like a bulldog, her chin aggressive.

Laura stood her ground beside Pat, longing to run away, yet determined to show no less courage than her companion.

Her question was greeted by a wild burst of laughter. One of the men swayed forward in a lurching fashion that betrayed his condition. 'We're on a treasure hunt,' he said thickly. 'You're our fourth clue.' He held up a sheet of paper which flapped about in the wind. 'We've got the policeman's helmet ...' waving a hand at the car, 'and the Keep Left sign. And the ...' He peered at the paper, screwing up his eyes. 'Oh, yes, the doctor's plaque ... Now we need an item of clothing from the first female we meet ...' He read the words off his list unevenly, then looked at them, grinning. 'That's you ... one of you ...'

He was a young man of medium height, his hair a rough brown mass of curls, his shoulders broad under his evening jacket.

Pat's voice was calm and not unfriendly. 'Medical students on a rag?' she asked.

He focussed on her. 'Good lord! Dracula's mother!'

Pat flushed angrily, stiffening.

One of his companions stepped forward at that moment, his gait measured enough for him to be almost sober. His voice was flippant to the point of insolence, yet the other three all turned to look as he spoke.

'I think we'd better look elsewhere. These ladies don't appear to be very co-operative.'

The first young man shook his head violently. 'No, no ... damn it, Randal, there's no time to be choosey. We've got to take what the gods send. It's in the rules. First female we meet ...' He looked at Pat again. 'Well, we've got a choice, so it isn't her ...' His eyes turned on Laura, who shrank back until she stood under the lamp, her green eyes as bright and angry as those of a cat in the yellow light. She was wearing a grey coat with a fur hood which half hid her face, but her slender figure was outlined rather than concealed by the tight-fitting cut of the garment.

The three younger men whistled admiringly. The brown-haired one jumped forward and pushed back her hood. Lamplight glinted on her silvery fine hair, turning it to bright gold.

'Good lord, she's a raving beauty!' the young man said with awestruck enjoyment. 'No contest, is there?'

Laura glared up at him, striking his arm away as he reached for her. 'Let me go, you drunken oaf!'

He gurgled with amusement. 'That's not a Cockney accent,' he declared. 'What on earth are you doing around here?'

'I'm the local social worker,' snapped Pat, stepping closer to Laura protectively. 'And if I call out there'll be a dozen strong-armed dockers out here in two minutes, so if I were you I'd get out of here now.'

The young man laughed. 'Not before I claim our clue,'

he said cheerfully, turning back to Laura.

Suddenly the least drunk of the quartet intervened, shouldering him out of the way. 'My privilege, I fancy,' he drawled in that insolent voice.

'If you touch me I'll scream the place down!' Laura said furiously, backing until she came up against the lamp-post, feeling it hard and cold against her back.

Staring up, she met pale grey eyes which seemed to pin her to the post as they surveyed her unwaveringly. A long-fingered hand came up to touch her hair gently, then the other hand seized her head and held it tilted up so that the light shone directly on to her face. 'I'll take one of your gloves,' he drawled. 'And this ...'

Before she realised his intention he bent and kissed her, his mouth cold from the night air, just brushing her lips at first, then suddenly seeming to take fire.

Pulling her into his arms, he clamped her hands at her side, his kiss suddenly hard and hot, wringing from her a faint, distressed sob. She could feel his tall, lean body pressing against her and hear a drumming of pulses, but she could not be sure whether it was her own heart beating or his.

He lifted his head after what seemed an eternity. Trembling, breathless, bitterly angry, she looked up at him. A slow smile twitched the corners of his hard mouth.

'You don't look as if you disliked that,' he said mockingly.

She hated his handsome, smiling face so much that she struck at him fiercely.

She was no longer even aware of the others watching them. A core of stark silence encapsulated herself and this man who had aroused in her emotions she had never experienced before and to which she could only respond with involuntary violence.

He jerked back his head as her hand flew out, but her blow connected, leaving an angry scratch running from his mouth to his tough jaw. It did not seem to anger him. He merely smiled again, so that she felt, confusedly, that he had actually enjoyed provoking her to such a gesture.

He lifted his hand and touched the cut. As his hand dropped she saw blood smeared on his finger. 'You've left your mark on me, my dear,' he said in a voice so soft it made her shiver in sudden terror.

'You're frightening her,' Pat said angrily at her shoulder. 'Leave the girl alone, can't you?'

The other men laughed, half embarrassed, half gleeful. 'Don't forget the glove,' cried one.

The man called Randal smiled. Without haste he removed the glove from Laura's hands, leaving her holding just one. Then he turned and moved back to the car without another glance. The other three followed him, whooping, and the engine raced. A moment later the car was gone and the two girls were alone.

Pat looked at Laura, half anxious, half irritated. 'I told you it was dangerous for you to come down here!'

Laura was still having difficulty with her breathing. Her voice husky, she said, 'They weren't residents, were they?' She gave a wild, half hysterical crack of laughter. 'What one might call carriage trade ...'

Pat scowled. 'All the same, I know who'll get the blame. Tom will be furious with me for exposing you to something like that.'

'I'm twenty years old,' said Laura passionately. 'Old enough to make up my own mind. I'm not a child.'

'Tell Tom that,' Pat said flatly. 'Oh, come on. I'll get you home ...'

Emerging on to a well-lit main road, they caught a bus to the rather more expensive part of town in which Laura lived, and then walked along a wide, tree-lined avenue until they reached the gate of her home.

'Will you be all right now?' Pat asked offhandedly.

'Yes, thank you,' Laura said shyly. 'Thank you for taking me tonight. I'm sorry you disapproved, but I'm not sorry I went.'

'I shan't take you again,' Pat warned. 'Tom will have my job for this as it is. I must have been insane to agree to it.'

'Why did you?' Laura asked curiously.

Pat flushed. 'I thought it would do you good to realise what a gulf there is between the sort of world you live in and the world Tom has chosen for himself.'

Laura looked at her closely, her face startled by a sudden suspicion, but she had no time to scrutinise Pat's face because the other girl turned and walked away down the road, her heels tapping on the pavement.

Laura let herself in at the front door and heard a voice calling to her anxiously from the long sitting-room which took up most of the ground floor of the house.

'Is that you, darling? Where have you been?'

She pushed open the door of the sitting-room and smiled at her mother. 'Pat and I went visiting.'

Mrs Hallam was a very small, very frail woman of about fifty; her white hair elegantly styled had once been the same ash-blonde shade as Laura's was now, and her eyes were the same soft green. Her health had always been delicate. Both her husband and her daughter spoiled and indulged her, yet she was remarkably unspoilt in her gentleness and selflessness. Occasionally she rebelled against the loving tyranny imposed upon her and insisted on a more active life, but her slight body had long ago been drained of strength, and any exertion brought on a weakness which terrified her family. The family doctor, a sensible Scot of middle years, had warned them that she must be forced to rest as much as possible or the results could be serious. She had suffered two heart attacks already, the last almost fatal. She might not survive another one.

Laura had devoted herself to her mother since leaving school. It had been her own choice. Mrs Hallam had protested at the idea, insisting that Laura should do something more interesting, but Laura had been determined, and with the doctor's backing was able to persuade her mother that she really wanted to stay at home. Secretly, Mrs Hallam had been relieved, Laura suspected, since if she had not stayed at home to look after her mother it would have been necessary to get a stranger to do it, and Mrs Hallam was both shy and nervous of strangers.

'Where is Dad tonight?' Laura asked, looking round the room with her usual feeling of pleasure. Mrs Hallam had a great gift for interior decorating. She had made the room both comfortable and charming. The warm mushroom colour of the walls, the sunny yellow of the curtains, combined extraordinarily well. The furniture was modern Scandinavian, well made and elegant.

'Your father is out,' said Mrs Hallam with a faint cloud passing over her face.

Despite his devoted love for his delicate wife, Mr Hallam had a passion for lively company that he could never resist indulging. He spent a great deal of time out with friends whom he rarely brought home. Gregarious by nature, he liked to enjoy his leisure hours in cheerful, noisy surroundings. His home was too quiet for him. When he did stay in, Laura had noticed, he seemed to grow melancholy after a while, as though the gentle ticking of the clocks and the peace of his wife's perpetual embroidery wore down his spirits.

Laura felt a spurt of unusual irritation. She would not have gone out tonight if she had not thought her father would stay with his wife. He had promised to do so. Why had he broken his word? How could he leave her mother alone like this?

'I think I'll go up to bed now you're in, dear,' said Mrs Hallam contendly, folding up her needlework. She occupied her time in making chair covers, tablecloths, napkins, all delicately and exquisitely embroidered with flowers and leaves.

'Shall I make you some hot milk?' Laura asked.

'Thank you, that would be very nice.' Mrs Hallam smiled at her affectionately. 'You know, we can always get a mother-sitter for the evening, if you ever want to go out, darling. Heaven knows, we can afford it. I hate to think of you staying at home night after night. You're young—you should have more fun than you do. It must be dull for you being so much at home.'

'Don't be silly,' Laura said gently. 'I love looking after you, and anyway, I do have fun. Tom takes me to the cinema once a week, if he can ...'

'If he can,' sighed her mother. 'But that isn't once a week, my dear. Not even once a month, I'm sure. Tom is so busy.' She gave Laura an anxious, hesitant look. 'A doctor's life is not an easy one, especially for his wife.'

Laura blushed. 'He hasn't asked me yet, Mother!' She

did not dispute the possibility, all the same. Her mother knew perfectly well how much Tom meant to her. She had never been able to hide anything from her mother.

'Tom is a very nice boy,' Mrs Hallam said carefully. 'He's a marvellous doctor and one of the kindest people I've ever met. But I would want you to think very carefully before you made any final decision about your future, Laura.' She smiled, her green eyes teasing. 'Oh, I know mothers are silly to interfere in their children's lives, and I'm probably only making you cross with me, but I can't help worrying about you ...'

Laura hugged her. 'I realise that. But you really have no need to worry, you know. Tom and I ...' She sighed. 'Tom has never even hinted at marriage yet. I'm pretty sure he thinks I'm much too young.' Her eyes lit with love. 'He still thinks of me as the little girl who used to tag along behind him everywhere when he was a medical student ...' The words suddenly reminded her of the earlier incident and her face went scarlet, as she remembered what had happened.

Mrs Hallam looked sharply at her. 'What is it? You've gone quite red.'

'Oh, just something that happened tonight,' Laura shrugged casually. 'We met some medical students doing a stunt of some kind ... playing silly tricks ... that's all.'

Mrs Hallam laughed. 'They all do it. Even Tom was quite wild as a student, although you wouldn't remember him in those days.'

Laura remembered Tom vividly from her earliest years, but she did not contradict her mother. Mrs Hallam turned away to go up the stairs and Laura went through into the kitchen to prepare her mother's hot milk. While she waited for it to heat she thought about the treasure hunters again, her face filled with burning anger and resentment.

The one who had kissed her, the one they had called Randal, had been much older than the rest. They, she judged, must have been more or less her own age; twenty or so. Randal could have been anything between thirty or forty—rather old to be indulging in wild adolescent behaviour.

She pressed her palms to her hot face, remembering with shame the wild impulses which had racked her when his hard mouth came down on her lips. It had never occurred to her before that there were impulses in her which did not answer obediently to the dictates of her mind and heart. What had leapt to life deep within her body during that kiss had been a blinding revelation, teaching her something about herself she had never known before, a dark fact which somehow changed her whole view of life.

In that moment she had recognised that her body had needs and desires which her love for Tom Nicol had never even touched, and it was that self-realisation which had driven her mad with rage and made her strike out at the man who had revealed her to herself so nakedly.

That her traitorous body should have responded to another man was bad enough, but that it should have been to a man she instinctively disliked had been unforgivable.

There was a hissing sound beside her, and she turned her dazed, uncomprehending eyes on the stove and saw that the milk had boiled over. Groaning irritably, she dealt with it and took the warm milk up to her mother, only to find her already fast asleep in bed, her face lit by the muted illumination of a bedside lamp.

Laura looked down on the tired, wan face with pity and love. Her mother had always been a delicate, gentle shadow in her life. She could remember how, as a child, she had been constantly afraid her mother would die. Tom's calm reassurance had been all that could comfort her at those times. Bending to kiss her mother's cheek, she switched off the lamp and tiptoed out.

She washed up the cup and made herself a cup of coffee, intending to go to bed at once, but as she moved into the hall her father let himself quietly into the house.

He looked startled and sheepish when he saw her. 'Oh, hallo, Laura,' he mumbled, forcing a smile.

'Dad, you shouldn't have gone out, leaving Mother alone,' she said quietly. 'What would have happened if she'd had an attack?'

He looked at her pleadingly. 'I only meant to go out for ten minutes, but I met someone and somehow time flew by ...' He looked like a penitent schoolboy as he gazed at her.

She sighed. 'I should never have gone out, I suppose ...'

His mood changed suddenly. He was a mercurial spirit, a creature of many moods. Now he looked sullen. 'I work very hard to give your mother the sort of home she needs,' he said, his lower lip pouting. 'It isn't easy working for the Mercier Company, you know. They expect a lot for their money, and that isn't over-generous, as I've told you. I need some relaxation when I get out of the office. I'm a human being, not a machine.' His eyes were self-pitying. 'But it would just suit that swine Mercier if I was a machine. He wouldn't need to pay me a penny, just switch me on and off and keep me well oiled.'

She had heard his complaints about his firm before. She looked at him with resigned affection. 'I know you work hard, Dad.'

'For peanuts, too,' he said in blustering tones.

Laura did not laugh, although the accusation was ridiculous. Whatever the Mercier company were like, they were not ungenerous, or how could her father manage to keep the substantial house they lived in, or buy his wife the beautiful, elegant clothes she always wore? There was always plenty of money in his pocket, even though he spent a great deal on the upkeep of the house.

James Hallam was a clever accountant. He had been employed by the Mercier firm for twenty years, and had risen rapidly in their company. A cheerful extrovert in his fifties, he had bright hazel eyes which smiled easily and a balding head of grey hair. He rarely talked about his work except to make generally disparaging remarks about his employer. All that Laura knew about the Mercier Company was what she had read in the papers.

Yves Mercier had landed in England some time after the first world war, a penniless French soldier. He had begun to work in one of the new car factories and later married the daughter of one of the partners who owned the business. Gradually over the next twenty years Mercier had acquired the whole business and branched out into several other manufacturing industries. He had two daughters and a son, who was now chiefly responsible for the running of the firm, and it had been since the son took over that James Hallam had begun to complain about his job there. Laura suspected that her father just disliked change. Young Mercier was a new broom and his energetic shake-up of the firm had offended her father.

James Hallam's mood suddenly changed again. With

an anxious look, he asked, 'Is your mother all right, then?'

She smiled at him reassuringly. 'She's fine. She was asleep when I looked in just now.'

He sighed, his shoulders relaxing. 'I don't think you realise what a strain her illness has been on me, Laura.'

'I do realise, Dad,' she said gently. She knew very well that he worshipped her mother. Anyone who had seen them together would have known that.

It was an odd marriage, all the same. James Hallam was so lively and extrovert, a man of bouncing noisy energy. His wife was gentle, quiet, delicate, fond of the peace of her own home and never wishing to have visitors. They seemed an ill-assorted couple, yet Laura knew they were happy together, despite her mother's long illness. The love between them was unmistakable.

Her father was frowning now. 'Do you think she looks any worse lately? I've thought once or twice that she was getting tired more quickly.'

'I don't think so,' Laura disclaimed at once. She would not even admit the possibility.

He smiled again, the shadow lifting from his face. 'That's good.' He glanced at her coffee. 'Mustn't let that get cold, Laura. Going to bed, were you?'

'Yes, Dad,' she said, reaching up to kiss him. 'Goodnight.'

She looked back as she reached the top of the stairs and was disturbed to see him look almost haggard as he stared into the shadows of the hall as if seeing ghosts.

Several times lately she had seen a similar expression on his face. Was it just worry over her mother? Or was something else troubling him? It was useless to ask him directly. He would not tell her. He had a certain vein of secretiveness which puzzled her.

She went into her bedroom and sat down on the edge of the bed to drink her coffee. It was lukewarm. She put it down half finished and began to get ready for bed.

Reading a detective novel later, she suddenly found her mind invaded by that insolent, dark face again. She made an angry noise, her eyes flashing.

How dared he kiss her like that?

The only man who had ever kissed her before was Tom, and his kiss had been gentle and comforting, bearing no resemblance whatever to the fierce instant possession the other man had taken of her lips.

Angrily she flung down her book and reached up to snap off the light. She would not allow him to dominate her mind a moment longer. He was not worth a second's thought, in fact. She would erase him and the memory of his kiss from her mind for ever.

If she could.

CHAPTER TWO

THE following morning Tom arrived to visit her mother. Although he was not her doctor he kept a careful watch over her health because they were distantly related and he had regarded Mrs Hallam as his aunt all his life. His mother was her second cousin, but remote though the connection might be, even a stranger could see a family resemblance between Laura, her mother and Tom Nicol. They had the same colouring, the same finely boned features, although Tom's hair was a warmer shade, something approaching the colour of melted honey, and his eyes were a gentle blue.

He was just past thirty, the son of a brilliant surgeon who had worked in the East End all his life out of choice, despite tempting offers from more well-heeled hospitals. There had never been any question but that Tom would follow in his father's footsteps. Medicine had fascinated him from an early age. He worshipped his father and was determined to model himself on him. Once he had qualified he set up in general practice in the East End. He had been deeply disappointed to find that he had been born without his father's clever, skilful hands and so could not become a surgeon. But in all else he was his father's son.

Laura's parents thought Tom was a fool to waste his talent in a rundown city district when he could have gone anywhere in the world. But Laura would never hear any criticism of him. To her he was perfect, the man she had adored and admired since she was a little girl.

She had not told him of her intention of visiting his district with Pat last night, uncertain of what his reaction would be. Now as he smiled at her she wondered if Pat had said anything to him. She knew they would have met earlier that morning. Pat visited his surgery several times a day to keep up the necessary contact between them on the cases they dealt with together.

'What's all this about you going out with Pat last night?' he asked quietly.

She looked at him uncertainly. He did not seem angry. But then Tom was not given to extremes of emotion. He carried around with him an armour of peaceful strength which he seemed to transfer to everyone he met, calming and soothing them even when they were in pain or distress. This was perhaps his most inestimable quality, and what made him already the most popular doctor who had ever worked in his part of London.

'I wanted to see where you worked,' she said hesitantly. 'I've heard so much about it, but I've never seen it ...'

Tom's blue eyes were troubled. 'You must promise me never to go there again,' he said slowly.

'Are you angry?' She was suddenly white, her mouth trembling. She could not bear it if he were angry with her.

'Angry?' His eyes scanned her uplifted face and one of his rare smiles lit his features. 'Have I ever been angry with you? How could anyone even frown at you when you look at him like that ...' His hand touched her cheek, stroking the smooth pale skin which was still bloomed with childhood and dusted with tiny almost invisible golden hairs.

Relief brought back her colour in a rush, turning her

a rosy pink, giving brightness back to her green eyes. She caught his hand and kissed it gently. Tom snatched it from her grasp with an almost angry gesture, then as she looked up at him again in bewildered alarm, smiled.

'You're getting too grown up to do things like that, darling,' he said gently.

Her lashes lowered, their gold tips glinting. Through them the green eyes peeped at him shyly. 'Don't you like me to kiss you, Tom?'

For a moment his face was filled with conflicting emotions, expressions she could not read and had never seen on his face before. Then he turned away, laughing. 'You little witch! Are you trying to flirt with me? You must be growing up ...'

'I am grown up,' she said crossly. 'I'm nearly twenty.'

'So old?' He mocked gently. 'And here was I thinking of buying you a doll for your birthday! I'll have to think again, won't I?'

'That's the trouble. You do think of me as a child,' she said passionately. 'I'm not—I'm a woman.'

His tired, sensitive face was a little teasing as he grinned at her. 'Never mind, darling. I'm sure there are young men ready to fall madly in love with you ...'

'I don't want young men falling in love with me,' she said with a faint break in her voice. Why was he being deliberately evasive? She knew he loved her. She could feel it every time he looked at her. His eyes caressed her with every glance. Why did he never say it, though? Why did he go on pretending to believe she was still a child? Surely her feelings had not deceived her? Could she be wrong about Tom's love?

'Well, there's plenty of time,' he said flatly. 'Don't be in too much of a hurry to grow up, will you?' He touched her cheek again, with an involuntary, half reluctant tenderness. 'I should be sorry to lose my little Laurie...' The pet name brought an answering smile from her.

'You'll never lose me, Tom,' she said eagerly. Was it possible that he did not know she loved him?

His hand dropped to his side stiffly, the fingers curled inwards towards the palm as though to control some action. 'Pat tells me you met a crowd of drunken students,' he went on quickly, his voice husky, 'And one of them kissed you. Were you frightened?'

'I was furious,' she said, but at the memory a surge of hot shame swept over her. She would never forgive herself for betraying Tom even for an instant. How could she have felt like that, have responded to that horrible man?

Tom's eyes were riveted on her face, watching the colour come and go, the green eyes brilliant with anger and self-contempt. He frowned, feeling for her hand. His long cool fingers discreetly touched her wrist, feeling for the pulse, finding it beating fast and strong beneath his fingertips.

'You can see why I don't want you wandering around that place at night,' he said. 'It's too risky. Anything could happen. There are muggings and rapes there all the time. You haven't been brought up to cope with that sort of world.'

She was touched by his concern, even though she resented the fact that Pat was allowed to share that part of his life while she was rigidly excluded. 'I promise not to go again,' she said. 'But I'm not made of sugar icing, Tom. I don't melt in the rain.'

He looked amused, his tired face lit with that tender smile. 'Don't you? Are you sure?' For a second something shone through his blue eyes that took her breath away. 'You're very special, Laurie. I couldn't bear it if anything hurt you. You're like a fragile piece of Dresden.' He held her wrist, raising it slightly. 'See, I can get two fingers round your wrist with room to spare. It would be a simple matter to break one of these tiny bird-like bones. You belong in another world, cherished and wrapped in cotton wool.' His voice was deadly serious now. 'My world is unlike anything you've ever known. Men kick their wives to death and beat their children, come home drunk and smash their furniture to bits. It's a violent, deadly world and I don't want any part of it ever touching you.'

'But, Tom ...' She wanted to say that she longed to share all of his world, even the violence and the fear, but he shook his head, cutting her off abruptly.

'Stay away from all that, Laurie.' Then he turned away and walked towards the stairs to go up and visit her mother, who was resting in her room.

Laura made some coffee while he was up there, but just as he came downstairs there was a loud ring at the door, and when she opened it her heart sank to see Pat standing there, square and aggressive in a dark brown coat, her sallow skin flushed by the cold weather.

'I've come to pick up Tom,' she said flatly. 'He's still here, I take it?' She glanced at her watch meaningly. 'We're in a hurry, so could you get him?'

Laura stepped back from the door, gesturing to her to pass. 'He's just coming.'

Tom reached the foot of the stairs as Laura closed the door. He smiled, nodding at Pat. 'Thanks for coming.' He looked at Laura. 'My car's out of action. I think there's some electrical fault. I've put it into the garage, but they say it will be two days before I get it back, so Pat is ferrying me around for the moment.'

Laura wished she had a car so that she could offer to help. Sighing, she said, 'I just made some coffee. Have you got time for a cup?'

Pat said quickly, 'No, sorry.'

Tom was watching Laura's mobile, expressive face. He gave a faint sigh. 'Oh, I think we could spare two minutes for some coffee, don't you, Pat? I'm dying for a cup, myself.'

Laura's face lit up joyfully. They followed her through to the kitchen and she poured the coffee, adding lots of cream to Tom's cup, so that he laughed and said teasingly, 'Hey! Are you trying to fatten me up?'

'You don't eat enough,' she said tenderly. 'You work too hard, and it's wrong to go without food for hours.'

Pat watched them expressionlessly. Tom was accepting his cup, his blue eyes fixed on Laura's delicate, fine-boned face. His face was filled with loving tenderness.

When he had quickly drained his cup, Tom reluctantly moved towards the front door. 'Goodbye, Laurie,' he said with a final glance. 'Take care of your mother.'

'If you take care of yourself,' she added softly with a brief glimmering smile.

Pat stumped past her, face glowering, and went to start the car. Tom got into the passenger seat. Suddenly Pat got out again and came back to the house.

She looked at Laura in an oddly aggressive way, as though defying her. 'I forgot to make an important phone call. Mind if I use your phone?'

'Of course not,' Laura said at once, indicating the door of the sitting-room. 'You know where it is.'

Pat went into the room, closing the door behind her.

Laura had time to run down to the car and lean on the window talking to Tom. 'You won't forget my birthday party, will you? You'll come? You have made arrangements for someone to take your calls?'

'Yes, I'll be there,' he said. 'Do you have any special wishes for your birthday? Anything you badly want?'

Her face grew pink. She laughed breathlessly. 'Dozens of things, I suppose ...' Then, seriously, 'No. I'll love whatever I'm given.'

'You're easy to please,' he said.

She glanced over her shoulder at the house. 'Pat doesn't think so. She thinks I'm spoilt.'

He did not deny it, but he said quickly, 'Pat doesn't know you. She'll realise what a mistake she's made one day.'

I doubt it, thought Laura. She had the feeling that Pat's dislike of her was basic, a rooted part of her character.

Then Pat was hurrying back, her face oddly flushed, her eyes full of a strange angry, scornful light. She dived into the car and started the engine without even looking at Laura. The car drew away. Tom glanced back once and his eyes met Laura's, resting on her face like a blessing.

She went back into the house and began to prepare her mother's lunch. Mrs Hallam got up, dressed and came downstairs at noon each day, by her doctor's orders. She was supposed to stay up just six hours, but she rarely kept rigidly to his rules because she liked to spend as much time as possible leading a normal life. The only part of his rules she liked to keep was the morning in bed, and Laura suspected that that was so that she would have plenty of time for herself while her mother was safely tucked up in bed. Mrs Hallam liked her to go out in the morning, take a nice walk through the local park. She worried constantly that Laura was not enjoying herself.

Lunch was a light one—fish in a white sauce followed by grapes. When they had eaten, Laura cleared away and washed up. Her mother came into the kitchen and picked up the tea towel.

'No, Mother,' Laura said firmly, taking it away from her.

'Darling, it can't hurt me to dry up a few plates!'

'Well, if you sit down while you do it ...' Laura conceded.

'I wish you wouldn't treat me as though I were a four-year-old,' Mrs Hallam complained. 'You're getting worse than your father.'

Laura looked at her, seeing the fragility of her small white face with concern. But she did not argue any longer, and Mrs Hallam dried up, chatting to her. 'Was that Pat Basset who came for Tom?' She made a face. 'Such a very blunt girl. I suppose it's a sign of honesty, but I sometimes feel she enjoys saying what she thinks instead of making up little white lies, like the rest of us.'

Laura laughed. 'Tom says Pat has integrity.'

'What's that supposed to mean?' her mother demanded. 'That she cares more about her own view of the world than the feelings of other people?'

'She does a wonderful job,' Laura said with a sigh. 'I could never be as brave as her. She really cares about the people she works with.'

'So she should,' said Mrs Hallam. 'Most people do, you know. She doesn't have the sole right to claiming that. We all get very involved with the people around us—that's what makes us human beings.' She moved towards the door. 'You do realise she's in love with Tom, don't you, darling?'

Laura froze, staring at her. 'W-why do you think that?'

'I've seen her looking at him,' Mrs Hallam said gently, watching her daughter's pale face. 'That's why she doesn't like you. Really, Laura, you're so naïve! Didn't that occur to you?'

Laura was not sure. Had she known? She had known from the start that Pat was hostile towards her. But that she should actually be in love with Tom ... that was a new idea. It was so incongruous. Pat was somehow almost asexual, her stocky, aggressive figure more masculine than feminine. Tom treated her in a comradely fashion. Laura had often seen him grin at her cheerfully, but he had never worn that special look which he wore when he sometimes looked at Laura.

She was not certain what made the look so special. A combination of tenderness and wistfulness, perhaps. It always made her feel warm and secure, as if his look wrapped her round with love.

When her mother was safely settled in a lounger chair, her embroidery begun, Laura went back into the kitchen to start the preparations for dinner. At three o'clock their daily help would arrive and Laura would be free to go out for an hour or two. Mrs Knight was always happy to keep an eye on Mrs Hallam while Laura did some shopping or took a walk.

They were having casserole for dinner. Laura peeled and diced vegetables, browned the meat quickly and soon had the large brown earthenware pot in the oven on a low heat.

ran upstairs to change. After the chilly weather

yesterday the temperature had gone up a little and the sun was making a brave attempt to shine in a cloudy blue sky. She searched through her wardrobe and found a warm light woollen dress in a soft turquoise shade. Over it she usually wore a white jacket. She swathed her silvery hair into a chignon at the back of her head, inspected herself critically and went downstairs.

Mrs Knight was on time, her round face beaming as Laura let her into the house. 'Going out? That's the ticket. I'll keep an eye on your mum, ducks. Off you go and have a nice time.'

'Thank you, Mrs Knight,' said Laura gratefully. 'I've got some of those chocolate ginger biscuits you like, for when you have your cup of tea.'

Mrs Knight looked pleased. 'That's very thoughtful of you. Thanks.'

Going in to say goodbye to her mother, Laura asked her if there was anything she could get her.

'Some of this yellow silk, darling, if you go near the shop,' said Mrs Hallam, snipping off a label and handing it to her. 'That's the number I need.'

Laura kissed her and went back to the front door. Just as she was opening it the door bell rang. She opened it and stared in surprise at the small boy standing on the doorstep.

'Yes?'

He was carrying a pale grey cardboard box with gold lettering printed on it.

'Miss Laura Hallam?' he asked in a hoarse voice.

She nodded. 'Yes.'

'A man asked me to give you this,' he said, handing the box to her.

Before she could question him he had gone. She stared

up and down the street, but there was no one in sight. She closed the door and looked at the box wonderingly.

Could it be an early present from Tom for her birthday? He had asked her what she wanted earlier. But why wouldn't he give it to her himself? It wasn't even her birthday for a fortnight.

She lifted the lid and gazed in delighted astonishment at the contents. On top of a pile of tissue paper lay a dark red rose. There was no card with it, but who else could have sent it but Tom? She picked it up carefully, inhaling the sweetness of the scent. Then she unwrapped the tissue paper, revealing a dozen pairs of gloves, all a different shade and material, all visibly very expensive.

Her face flamed. Suddenly she knew who had sent these, and it was not Tom.

How dared he? Did he think that this ludicrous, overwhelming gesture of apology could make any difference to the hatred and contempt she felt for him?

For a second she thought of throwing the gloves into the fire, then her fingers, as she snatched at them to do so, unconsciously lingered on the smooth, silky texture of them. She had never worn gloves like these. They were so finely made of the best materials.

She shrugged. After all, it would be stupid to destroy anything so beautiful. It would be making the man more important than he was. She would accept them in the spirit in which they had no doubt been sent—as an admission of his insolence last night.

A smile curved her lips as she searched through the gloves for a pair which would match her white jacket. She chose a pair and put the box carefully out of sight in the hall cupboard, then slipped out of the house.

The avenue led down to the park. She walked briskly,

her head high, enjoying the feel of the sunshine on her face. There were few people about at this time of day. Mothers with small children feeding the ducks on the lake. Men with dogs who pulled at their leads in an attempt to fight each other. Old people sitting on park benches watching the world go by.

Laura strolled along beside the lake, watching the ducks flap angrily at each other as they quarrelled over crumbs. The water glinted in the sunlight. A few brown leaves floated on the surface.

Someone laughed softly behind her. She turned, a smile on her own face, then froze as she recognised him.

A slow, mocking smile touched the corners of his hard mouth as he saw her expression.

'I see you're already wearing my gloves,' he drawled in that lazily ironic voice. 'I particularly liked that pair. The white kid was so smooth and virginal—it reminded me of you.'

Laura's cheeks flushed wildly and her eyes flashed. She pulled the gloves off her hands, resentfully aware of her own clumsiness and his watchful amusement, and flung them into the lake.

He laughed out loud. 'How passionate you are! A promising sign.'

She turned on her heel and walked away fast, hearing him stride after her. As she walked she wondered for the first time how he had found out her name and address. He drew level with her. She shot him a sidelong glance of loathing, marvelling that although they had only met once before she was already so hatefully familiar with the strong jawline, the windblown black hair, the powerful angular face. He was probably what some women would have called a handsome man, but to Laura his good looks were completely marred by his arrogant expression, and the curious glitter in the pale grey, mocking eyes which made her feel like running away in terror.

She stopped. 'Do I have to call that park keeper and tell him you're bothering me?'

'Am I bothering you?' he asked lightly.

She abandoned that discussion. She did not like the look on his face as he asked the question.

'How did you find out my name and address?' she asked instead.

He smiled quizzically. 'Your friend identified herself as a social worker, remember? It was easy to trace her. Once I knew where to find her it was easy to find you.'

She frowned. 'You followed her to my house, you mean?'

He shook his head. 'I went to her flat and asked her for your address.' The grey eyes narrowed thoughtfully. 'She refused to tell me, but later she rang me at work and had apparently changed her mind, because she gave it to me then.'

Laura remembered the phone call Pat had made, and her odd expression as she came out of the house. Why had Pat done it? She might have warned her that she had told him where to find her.

She turned away again. 'Please leave me alone. I don't want to talk to you.'

'That's a pity,' he said. 'Never mind.' His long legs kept an easy pace beside her.

She stopped again. 'Look, will you go away? I don't want to be rude, but you'll force me to be so if you don't leave me alone.'

'Don't you want to hear me apologise?' he asked softly.

DISTURBING STRANGER

She risked a look up at his face. Her eyes collided, with violent impact, with the cold grey gaze. Her pulses began to throb. What on earth is the matter with me? she asked herself angrily. Why does he disturb me so much?

'My nephew is a medical student,' he drawled. 'Last night they had a charity rag ball. The committee had organised that ridiculous treasure hunt as part of the fund-raising activities. I was roped in to give aid and comfort, so I drove Roddy and his friends around.'

'They were disgustingly drunk,' she accused, her blue eyes filled with contempt.

'That was precisely why I drove them,' he shrugged. 'I didn't want Roddy killing himself. My sister would never have forgiven me.'

'You were sober, of course,' she said sarcastically.

'I'd had a drink or two,' he drawled. 'I was far from being drunk, however.'

'You behaved as though you were,' she said coldly.

He smiled, the grey eyes mocking. 'Because I kissed you? I assure you I was never more conscious of what I was doing in my life.'

Laura felt a dizzy sensation at the words. Loathsome man, she thought. Why is he looking at me like that? Why had he deliberately sought her out? She felt his eyes on her face as though they were a brand, eyes which stamped her as his possession, making her tremble and want to run home as fast as she could.

'I thought you said you were going to apologise,' she flung at him. 'It doesn't sound like an apology to me.'

'I meant to apologise,' he murmured drily. 'But somehow I can't be sorry I kissed you, even though it must have alarmed you at the time. The sensation was far too delightful. I've been waiting ever since for the chance to do it again.'

Her skin coloured hotly. 'Well, you won't get the chance, believe me!' She abandoned her attempt to be cool and collected and ran headlong along the path, only to realise that she had gone the wrong way and was heading straight for the lonely path between a line of dark firs.

Alarmed, she halted and swung round, only to find him right behind her. They stared at each other. Laura was flushed and breathless, her eyes enormous. He was cool and intent.

'How old are you, for God's sake?' he asked.

'Twenty,' she said, chin lifted defiantly.

He raised one thin brow. 'You look about seventeen.' His hand shot out, taking her by surprise, curving around her chin and holding her head immobile. The grey eyes skimmed over her face.

'You really are exquisite,' he said as if to himself. 'Your skin is perfect, your hair is an incredible colour ... like spun silver ... your eyes are remarkable, the exact colour of the spring.' His other hand moved up to trace her features, his fingers sensitive and cool. 'Laura,' he said, his tongue lingering on the name. 'Yes, it suits you.'

She was hypnotised, held in his grip, although he exerted no real pressure, by the compelling grey eyes. Was he going to kiss her again? she wondered feverishly, and shivered as she realised she actually wanted him to.

'Laura,' he said again, very softly.

His head moved closer. His face loomed larger and larger. She was dry-mouthed with excitement, her heart thudding.

His lips touched hers at last. Her eyes stayed open staring at the sky, feeling a terrifying sweetness engulf her.

The kiss was light, very brief, bearing no resemblance to the passionate kiss of last night.

'There,' he said softly. 'That wasn't so horrifying, was it?'

She swallowed. 'I hate you,' she said on a smothered sob.

He laughed, incredibly, his grey eyes filled with laughter. 'That's a shame when I've just told you how I admire you.'

'I don't want your admiration!'

'No, I know you don't,' he said, smiling oddly, gazing at her with a curious little flicker in his eyes. 'I suspect that's what makes you so attractive to me. It's always more exciting to pursue a quarry which is in full flight. Easy prey are boring.'

Laura shivered again. The thread of ruthless power in his drawling voice alarmed her.

'Why won't you leave me alone?' she almost wailed.

'Ah,' he said softly. 'Having once set eyes on that enchanting little face, how could I? Any red-blooded male would find you irresistible.' His eyes narrowed. 'Is there a rival in the background somewhere?' He surveyed her closely. 'That was an idea that hadn't occurred to me until now.'

She looked away, her lashes fluttering to veil her eyes. 'I'm not going to talk about my private life to you!'

'That means there is someone,' he nodded. 'Well, I'll soon find out. Will you have dinner with me tonight?'

'Certainly not!'

'Lunch tomorrow?'

She shook her head.

'No polite excuses?' he teased.

'I don't want to,' she said pointedly.

He laughed, not a whit put out. 'Never mind, I'll find some other way of getting to you.'

The threat filled her with nameless terror. 'What do you want from me?' she asked shakily.

His brows lifted. 'My dear, you're not that young!' He ran his lazy grey eyes over her slight, curved figure. 'You know very well what I want.'

Again the colour ran up her face and her eyes widened as if he had struck her. She felt like a hunted animal under the possessive stare of his eyes.

'You're insane,' she cried breathlessly.

His mouth curved mockingly. 'I think I must be,' he agreed. 'I've never wanted anything as much as I want you, and I warn you, my dear, I've never failed to get what I want.'

'Then this will be a new experience for you,' she said in angry repudiation.

'No,' he said lazily, grinning at her. 'It will be a new experience for you. You have a lot to learn, Laura Hallam, and I shall enjoy teaching you.'

She turned and ran at that, and this time he did not follow her.

CHAPTER THREE

THE next time Pat came to call for Tom after his visit to Mrs Hallam, Laura faced her directly with the question, 'Why did you give that man my address?'

Pat flushed darkly. 'He said he wanted to apologise.'

Laura's blue eyes surveyed her thoughtfully. 'Did you really believe that?'

'What else?' Pat said, her eyes evasive.

Just then Tom came down and Laura dropped the subject. Watching Pat as she talked to Tom, it was obvious now that Mrs Hallam's suspicion was correct. Pat was in love with Tom. Her eyes lit up as she looked at him and she was pitifully aware of him all the time. Laura felt a qualm of sadness for her. She was convinced that Tom felt nothing towards Pat but friendship. He had never shown any sign of a warmer feeling.

But then had he ever shown any sign towards herself? Anxiously she studied his features, seeking for some clue in them. What did Tom really feel?

The long-standing relationship they had always shared obscured the truth. If Tom had begun to feel a more personal interest in her, he had no intention of showing it. Just then he looked round and their eyes met. His face lit with that rare, tender smile he only ever showed to her, and her body melted with tremulous happiness.

'Why are you looking so serious, my darling?' he asked her softly. 'I don't like to see you frown. You'll make lines on your pretty forehead.'

Pat's face darkened. She stared down at her hands.

'Did you think Mother looked well today?' Laura asked evasively.

Tom sighed. 'As well as she ever looks.' His eyes were anxious as he looked back at her. 'Like you, your mother is fragile. She needs to be taken care of.'

'I take care of her,' she said, pricked with faint resentment.

'I know you do,' he said quickly. 'I wasn't being critical. You're wonderful with her. But we must be vigilant, Laura. She needs to be watched.'

Laura nodded. 'I realise that. Today she sneaked out and began pruning the roses. Luckily I caught her at it before she'd been out there long.'

He groaned. 'She's naughty. I've warned her about it. Her heart just can't take any strain. She's living on the end of a fine thread. One more jerk and it will snap.'

Laura was pale, her eyes dark with anxiety. Tom touched her cheek briefly. 'Don't worry, we'll keep her alive despite herself.'

After he and Pat had gone Laura went to find her mother. She was amused to find her eating a humbug—Mrs Hallam had a passion for the sweets, as Tom was aware, and he sometimes brought her a few in a paper bag, although her diet was strictly controlled.

Mrs Hallam looked at her guiltily. 'Just one, darling. It won't hurt.'

'Tom spoils you!'

'He spoils both of us,' Mrs Hallam said, smiling.

That evening James Hallam came home whistling, his face wreathed in smiles. 'Guess what!' he said as he kissed his wife. 'We've had an invitation!'

She raised a curious look to his face. 'Invitation to what?'

'You remember I told you that some of the senior staff have been invited to a party at the Mercier house?'

'Yes,' she nodded. Then her eyes widened. 'You don't mean that you've been invited?'

He nodded, delighted. 'Not only me ... my whole family. The invitation is for all of us.'

'But I couldn't go,' said Mrs Hallam in alarm. Then her eyes grew wistful. 'Could I?'

'I don't see why not. We'll ask Tom,' he said. 'You must have a new dress, Laura. This is a very special occasion. Old Mercier has a fabulous house, they say. I've always wanted to see it, but this is the first time any of the staff have been invited. I was amazed when I got my invitation card. Some of our department have been invited, but I hadn't had a card, so I thought I wasn't one of the lucky ones. Then it came today and I was really excited.'

'When is it?' Laura asked.

'Tomorrow night,' he said. 'So you must hurry up and buy that new dress, mustn't you? Now get something stunning. I want to be proud of my little girl.'

Mrs Hallam smiled at Laura. 'If I can't come, Mrs Knight will be glad to come round and stay with me, darling, so don't worry about that.'

'You must have a new dress, too,' James Hallam said quickly. 'Laura will help you buy it.'

'I've got a perfectly good dress to wear if I go,' she said, shaking her head. 'That green dress, remember? I only wore it once at the annual dance.'

'Oh, yes,' he nodded. 'That was a lovely dress. Yes, wear that, darling.'

But Tom, as Laura had suspected, was regretfully forced to say that her mother could not go. Privately he said, 'The excitement would be too much for her. She had a very rapid pulse as it is when I got here. Just the thought of the party was having its effect. I shudder to think what the party itself would do to her. No, she can't go. Out of the question.'

Mrs Hallam bore the disappointment well. She was accustomed to her isolation by now. And of course, she had never been as gregarious as her husband.

Laura went out next morning to buy a new dress. She chose a bewitching sea green chiffon, full-skirted and tight-waisted, the style simple but very pretty on her slender figure. The bodice was a trifle low, but the assistant who sold it to her seemed to find it perfectly acceptable, although Laura felt a little exposed in it.

Mrs Knight arrived in time and James Hallam kissed his wife goodbye, half ashamed to be so excited at going out when she had to stay behind. Mrs Hallam looked at Laura for a long moment, her eyes bright.

'You look lovely, darling,' she said.

Laura smiled, grateful for the compliment.

They drove across London into that district which is the exclusive prerogative of the rich, the white stone canyons of those Mayfair streets with their slim porticoes and rows of flat windows. James Hallam drew an envious breath as he parked.

'The Merciers certainly have a wonderful life. Look at that house!'

Laura looked dispassionately. It was beautiful, she admitted, but she did not envy the people who lived in it. The frontage was long for a London house, built of

Portland stone, with a row of shallow stone steps leading up to the portico.

They rang the bell and waited. A butler opened the door, his bald head erect.

James Hallam proudly offered him his invitation card. The man bent a supercilious gaze upon the small square of card, then without a word he stood back to let them pass.

The hall was long and lofty, the walls half-panelled in oak, the floor tiled with polished satinwood which reflected them as they walked over it.

The butler took their coats with the glazed expression of someone doing a job he resents, then he led them through into a long, exquisitely furnished room.

It was filled with people standing about with drinks in their hands and expressions of polite anxiety on their faces. Several of them stared in surprise at James Hallam, who was flushed and nervous.

Laura moved closer to her father, studying the other guests, wondering which one was their host.

Suddenly her eye fell on an all-too-familiar face and she caught her breath in amazement.

He moved towards them, a smile lifting the corners of his hard mouth. Laura felt herself begin to tremble. Did he work for the same company as her father? What a ghastly coincidence!

Then she saw her father beaming, heard him say obsequiously, 'Good evening, Mr Mercier.'

And her eyes flew wide in disbelief and all the colour left her face.

She heard that loathsome voice drawl something, then her father turned to her and said, 'Laura, my dear—Mr Randal Mercier. This is my daughter, sir.'

Dazedly she saw the hand held out to her. Somehow she put out her own. She felt the cool fingers take possession of her hand and hold it, then, amazingly, he bent, lifting her hand, and kissed the back lightly.

'This is a delightful surprise,' he drawled. 'Mr Hallam, you have a very beautiful daughter.'

She snatched her hand away, made dizzy by the touch of his mouth on her skin, and pushed it down the side of her dress, as though to obliterate the print of his kiss.

He smiled, flickering one thin brow upward. Standing so close he could see quite clearly the expression in her blue eyes.

He turned back to her father. 'My father has been looking forward to meeting you again, Mr Hallam. He's over there. Why don't you join him? I'll get your daughter a drink.'

Laura wanted to cry out in protest, but she dared say nothing. Her father, looking delighted, moved away and she was left alone with Randal Mercier.

He looked down at her, the long nose supercilious. 'I told you I always get my own way,' he drawled.

'Why didn't you tell me you were my father's employer?' she demanded. 'You knew when we met in the park, didn't you? Pat told you.'

'If I had told you, would you have been nicer to me?' he asked drily.

'No,' she said angrily.

He smiled. 'Then why should I tell you? You wouldn't have come tonight if you'd known I would be here, would you?'

It was true. She looked away, silently acknowledging the fact, and he laughed.

'I can read your every expression, my dear. You have a

very expressive face. What would you like to drink?'

'Nothing,' she said flatly.

He did not argue. Taking possession of her elbow, he steered her out of the room, past little groups of curious people who stared at her discreetly and whispered to each other. Laura caught one remark, uttered sotto voce. 'Randal's found a new butterfly for his collection ... pretty little thing, isn't she?'

She flushed angrily and he looked down at her sideways. 'What is it?'

They were in the hall now. She was able to wrench her arm from his grasp now they were no longer being watched.

'Why have you brought me out here?' she demanded.

His hard mouth dented humorously. 'I'm not planning to rape you, if that's what's on your mind.'

'It isn't on my mind,' she said angrily.

His glance grew suddenly passionate. 'It's on mine,' he said, taking her breath away.

Her face flamed. 'How dare you?'

He laughed. 'You're very predictable, Laura Hallam.' He took hold of her hand firmly. 'I'm going to take you up to meet my mother. She's bedridden or she would have come down to meet you.'

Her eyes grew puzzled. Why did he want her to meet his mother? He read her bewildered face and a wry smile touched his mouth.

'My mother, like myself, collects beautiful things,' he said lightly. 'She's wanted to meet you ever since I told her how lovely you were.'

'You told your mother about me?' She could not believe it.

He grinned. 'Not quite everything,' he said wickedly.

Laura looked down, her pulses fluttering. He began to walk towards the stairs and she, perforce, went with him, her hand still held firmly in his.

He opened a bedroom door and waved her forward into the room. Lying in a large fourposter bed was a grey-haired woman with the same piercing grey eyes and angular features as Randal Mercier. She looked across the room at Laura with obvious interest.

'Come here, my dear,' she said in a pleasant voice.

Laura obediently crossed the room and stood beside the bed. The lamplight fell on her face as the woman moved her lamp. Grey eyes looked at her from a lined, pain-worn face.

'Yes,' sighed Mrs Mercier, 'she's all you said, Randal. Very lovely. How old are you, my dear?'

'Nearly twenty,' Laura whispered shyly.

Mrs Mercier's eyes smiled at her. 'You look younger. Tell me about yourself. Your father works for the firm?'

Laura nodded.

'And your mother?'

'My mother is delicate,' Laura said, her face clouding with sadness. 'She has a weak heart.'

Mrs Mercier made a face. 'I sympathise with her. I've been unable to get out of this bed for five years, except to sit in a wheelchair. I had a crash in my car one day and from being a perfectly fit, energetic woman I've become a helpless vegetable.'

'Hardly that, Mama,' Randal said in his teasing voice. 'You exercise complete control over the house and family from your bed, as you know perfectly well ...'

'I've never had any control whatsoever over you, Randal,' his mother said. 'You mustn't tell the child lies.'

Randal glanced at Laura, his eyes filled with laughter.

'She doesn't believe a word I say anyway, Mama. You have no need to warn her.'

Mrs Mercier laughed. 'She sounds remarkably level-headed. It's always annoyed me that women find you so devastatingly attractive. It has undoubtedly ruined your character. Even a man without vanity would have his head turned by all the adoring women who've pursued you over the years, and you, Randal, have never been free from vanity.'

He lifted a thin brow. 'Are you joining the enemy, Mama? Laura already believes me to be vain. Don't encourage her.'

Mrs Mercier glanced at Laura. 'I can see you're a good judge of character, Laura. Randal needs to be reminded from time to time that he's not God. He has too much power and too much money.'

'I shall take her away again if you're going to put words into her mouth,' Randal said.

'I'm merely giving her my opinion.'

'You're arming her for battle against your own son, you mean,' he retorted. 'Unfair, Mama. She has too many weapons as it is!'

Mrs Mercier looked back at Laura, who was listening in complete bewilderment to this exchange. A smile touched the older woman's mouth. 'We're frightening the child.' She frowned. 'She's very young, Randal.'

He took Laura's arm. 'Say goodnight to my mother,' he commanded.

Laura confusedly murmured, 'Goodnight, Mrs Mercier. It was nice to meet you ...'

Mrs Mercier watched her leave the room with a slight frown on her strong, handsome face.

On the landing Randal looked down at Laura, his

brows lifted. 'What did you think of my mother?'

'I liked her,' Laura said directly. 'She's honest and plain-speaking.'

'She's as cunning as a crocodile,' Randal said with a grin. 'And as devious as a crab. But you're too young to recognise it.'

'I'm not a child,' she snapped. 'Stop talking above my head!'

He laughed. 'Did I sound patronising?'

'Yes,' she said resentfully.

He led her down the stairs and opened a door she had not seen before. She halted, wary and surprised. 'Aren't we going back to the party?'

He jerked on her hand, pulling her into the room, and closed the door, leaning his back against it.

Laura backed away, her heart beating fast beneath the green chiffon. Something in the way he watched her made her tremble.

'We're wasting time,' he said softly. 'Come here.'

'I will not,' she said defiantly.

He gave a slow, amused smile. 'Do you want me to come and get you?'

She looked around her in nervous apprehension, but saw no way of escape. The room was furnished in a modern, functional style with leather armchairs, shelves of books, a large desk and some stark modern paintings on the walls.

With the soft tread of a panther he came towards her. She backed, shivering with fear and expectation.

As his hands closed on her slender shoulders she gave a gasp of sheer terror, throwing him a pleading glance. 'No, please, don't ...'

It seemed to annoy him. His brows drew together and

the grey eyes lost their teasing smile.

'I'm not an ogre, for God's sake,' he snapped.

She struggled in his grasp, her slight body swaying sideways. 'Will you let me go?' she demanded, her temper rising.

'I'm damned if I will,' he said tightly. He suddenly moved, picking her up into his arms as if she were a doll. Taken aback, she clung to his shoulders to steady a dizziness which was sweeping over her, and at that moment he bent his head and kissed her, his hard mouth compelling a response.

Walking with her to a deep leather armchair, he sat down, his mouth still bruising her lips, and settled her comfortably across his lap, her head cradled against his arm.

Her eyes were closed tight, she still clung to his shoulders. The long kiss went on and on until she was breathless, then he raised his head.

He was flushed and unsmiling as he looked down at her. 'That's better,' he said softly.

She hated herself for her weakness. How did he manage to make her submit? She had been determined not to let him kiss her, yet he had, and she had not only let him, she had responded passionately. She could not pretend to herself that it had all been on his side; she knew that the kiss had been mutual.

She lowered her lashes, looking at him through them, tracing the strong outline of the handsome face. He was watching her as intently, a smile playing around his mouth.

'You enchant me,' he said abruptly, his voice hoarse.

Her lids flew up in astonishment and she stared at him, wide-eyed.

Was he actually saying that he was in love with her? She looked at him in unconscious calculation, the idea dazzling in its novelty. It was an exciting thought. She would not be able to resist the pleasure of holding such a whip over his sleek black head. There was something satisfying in the idea of having power over such a very powerful man.

His grey eyes had narrowed, and a wry smile curved his mouth. 'You look very pleased with yourself,' he drawled. 'I think you've misinterpreted my meaning, though. You're premature if you imagine you've added my scalp to your collection. I merely meant that you were an enchanting creature and I would very much like to make love to you.'

She gasped, red-cheeked. Did he mean ...? She stared furiously at him. 'If you think that I ... that I would let you ... you're the most insolent man I've ever met!'

One cool hand lifted her chin, pushing back her head. 'A pity,' he drawled. 'You're so very desirable.'

Laura slapped his hand away, scrambling to get up.

He permitted her to do so and stood up himself, catching her hand as she turned to leave the room. 'Not yet,' he said.

'Let me go or I swear I'll scream the place down,' she said. 'I don't think you'd like that. The publicity would be embarrassing for you, wouldn't it?'

He grinned, unalarmed. 'I've got something to ask you,' he said. 'Will you have dinner with me tomorrow?'

Her glance was scornful. 'I've told you once. No.'

He shrugged. 'I should have thought that by now you would realise that I always get my own way. It would be far simpler if you just gave in, Laura.'

'I've never had an ambition to be anyone's mistress,' she said coldly.

He laughed. 'Pity, you would fill the role so delightfully.'

She glared at him. 'What do you think my father would say if he knew the sort of suggestion you've just made to me?'

He looked amused. 'I imagine he would be very shocked,' he said. 'Are you going to tell him?'

She eyed him resentfully.

'You know that if I do, he'll leave your firm,' she said icily. 'And then what will happen to him? He's over fifty. He'd be unlikely to get another job at his age, certainly not one as good, anyway.'

Randal Mercier grinned. 'You look very pretty when your eyes flash like that,' he said. 'I had a cat with eyes that colour once.'

'I hope she scratched you!'

His eyes laughed at her. 'She did. I've never been deterred by a little healthy hostility. In fact, I find it exciting.'

Their eyes duelled. Laura looked away, her heart pounding. Why did he look at her like that, his glance taunting and teasing her, making her go weak at the knees for some reason she did not care to investigate?

He moved closer, sliding his hand along the naked white curve of her throat until it cupped her chin. She stiffened and tried to move away, but his other hand came up to clamp her to his body so that she could not get away from him without a struggle.

'Would you kindly let me go?' she demanded, her green eyes bright with temper.

'On one condition,' he whispered, his breath warm against her cheek.

'Well?' she asked, leaning back slightly to avoid his intruding mouth.

'Kiss me,' he murmured, his mouth at once finding her exposed throat. 'Just one kiss freely given and I'll let you go ...'

'You're intolerable!' she snapped, pushing at his broad shoulders, her body twisting to escape his arms.

His mouth travelled down to the hollow of her throat where her pulse beat frantically. She found the sensation unbearably exciting. No one had ever done such things to her before. There was an intimate quality about the situation which left her breathless.

He stopped kissing her throat and raised his face, wiped clean of all expression. The grey eyes challenged her. 'Well?'

She leaned forward and kissed the hard, arrogant mouth briefly.

'Cheat,' he said softly. 'That wasn't a kiss—it was a promise.'

'You said you'd let me go,' she accused him.

'I said a kiss,' he shrugged. 'A real kiss, not a peck.'

Angrily she leant forward and kissed him hard. At once his lips parted, his arms pulled her nearer and she heard again that rapid drumbeat of a heart in the grip of excitement. Was it his? Or hers?

They swayed together, their bodies so close she could still not determine whose was that out-of-control heartbeat. A fiery urgency seemed to carry her away, as if a storm had blown up inside her, tearing her from her moorings, blowing her like a leaf on the wind. His hands moved and she heard herself gasp against his mouth.

His lips drew back a little, then bore down on her again hungrily, and she surrendered, weak and pliant, no longer disputing the right of those hard, compelling, expert hands to move where they wished.

When the excitement ended she was lost, her eyes blind and closed against the light, her hands clinging to him. If he let her go she would fall down.

At last she opened her eyes to find him watching her like a cat at a mousehole.

'End of lesson one,' he said mockingly.

Laura could have hit him. Instead she pulled herself away and went angrily to the door. Over her shoulder she said coldly, 'You can forget the other lessons, teacher. I've decided the subject bores me.'

He laughed aloud, his grey eyes full of glinting amusement. 'You're a very responsive pupil,' he murmured.

She went scarlet, then white, opened the door and went out, slamming it behind her.

She found her father in the other room and joined him quietly, standing there like a dutiful daughter, but constantly on the alert for Randal to appear. When he did she knew he had come, even though she did not look round. Her hammering pulses warned her.

The evening wore on endlessly. She could not leave until her father was ready to go, and he was enjoying every second of this party. A glass permanently in his hand, he talked easily to the other guests, laughing, telling jokes, listening with interest to the others.

This was his favourite way of passing time. He could not be happier if he tried.

Suddenly her leaping pulses told her Randal was close behind her. She dared not look round. She swallowed, trembling convulsively.

'Good evening again, Mr Hallam,' he said just behind her shoulder.

Her father looked at him cheerfully. A little flushed, a little unsteady on his feet, James Hallam had had too much to drink. 'Ah, Mr Mercier,' he said thickly. 'Marvellous party ... all enjoying it very much ...'

'I'm very glad to hear it,' Randal said politely. 'We must do it more often. It's pleasant to get to know the staff on a more personal basis.'

James Hallam was delighted. His old hatred for 'that swine young Mercier' quite forgotten, he said he thought that a great idea. 'And you must come to dinner with us some time,' he said as an afterthought.

'Thank you,' said Randal. 'I'd like that very much.' He drew a diary out of an inside pocket and flipped over the pages. 'I'm very busy, of course ...'

James stared at him dimly, trying to focus. He could not quite believe this.

'I'm afraid the only evening I have free is tomorrow,' Randal said smoothly. 'I suppose that wouldn't give you time to make preparations?'

The other guests hid smiles, believing Randal to be discreetly avoiding having dinner with the Hallams. James Hallam raised his chin belligerently.

'Certainly not,' he said thickly. 'Delighted if you come tomorrow. Aren't we, Laura?'

Laura was aghast, her body held rigidly, her face pale. She moistened her lips with a dry tongue. 'Of course,' she said somehow, her throat parched.

'Delighted ...' James Hallam repeated, frowning at her for not sounding more enthusiastic.

Randal blandly wrote something in his diary. 'That

will be very pleasant,' he said. 'I look forward to tomorrow.'

Laura risked a glance at him, her eyes burning with hatred and temper.

He gave her one of his lazy, mocking smiles and half bowed. Then he had moved away.

At last it was time to go. The party was breaking up. Laura was worried about her father. He was in no condition to drive home, but she dared not ask if she might phone for a taxi for fear Randal might overhear and offer to drive them home. She could not bear to be alone with him again.

As she and her father moved stumblingly to the door, however, the butler murmured discreetly, 'A taxi is waiting for you, miss.'

'For me?' She frowned. 'Are you sure you have the right person?'

'Yes, Miss Hallam,' he said with a very slight smile. 'The master asked me to ring for one.' He gave her father a passing glance. 'He thought you might need it.'

Laura flushed hotly and looked back into the half deserted room. Randal, leaning against the mantelpiece, a glass in one long hand, his manner languidly casual, was watching her and gave a slight, ironic bow in recognition of her.

She knew a moment's angry hatred of him. How dared he see and pass judgment on her father's weakness? He thought himself omniscient. Wasn't that what his mother had meant when she said he thought he was God? He seemed to have a comprehensive knowledge of human nature, but very little generosity. He had looked at her and desired her; her cheeks burnt bitterly in the taxi home as she thought about that. His determined, ruthless pursuit of her was an insult. He meant to possess her—he had as good as told her so. He did not even pretend to be emotionally involved with her. It was sheer blackmail, the way he had got her father to invite him to dinner, knowing she dared not protest.

Oh, he was clever! Shrewd, powerful, sophisticated, he knew what he wanted and went straight to get it, not caring what happened to those in his way.

She hated herself, despised herself, for having found him irresistibly attractive. Why did he have this power over her? What was wrong with her, that, loving one man, she could be so easily seduced by another?

She thought of Tom with longing, her eyes dreamy as she visualised his sunny hair and quiet, tender eyes. Tom was quite different, a man she could respect and admire, even hero-worship. Comparing him with Randal Mercier she felt sick.

It Tom ever found out how she had behaved in that room just now he would despise her.

She tried to make sense out of it. She did not love Randal Mercier, so why did her body melt when he touched her? Why did the descending nearness of that hard mouth make her weak with hunger?

She shivered. Even now the thought of it made her head swim. She sat up, staring into the dark streets. Her father had fallen asleep, his head lolling on his chest.

Perhaps, she thought suddenly, her love for Tom had made her vulnerable to Randal Mercier's physical attraction? Tom had never even really kissed her. Indeed, she had never felt anything like that with Tom. She knew that her love for him was pure and deep, true as sounding iron. The way she felt about Tom had no taint of the fevered, dizzying ecstasy Randal Mercier had aroused in her.

I'll never let him near me again, she thought bitterly. I'm warned now. I know his intentions and I surely have enough will power, enough self-respect, to fight the response he arouses in me against my will.

Yet despite her brave intentions, her spirits were low as she got into bed that night and it was a long time before she fell asleep.

CHAPTER FOUR

NEXT morning, after her father had left for the office, she went up to her mother's bedroom to talk to her about the dinner party, and found her sitting up in bed against her piled pillows, poring over a cookery book. Laura considered her with a grin. 'Dad's told you, I see?'

Mrs Hallam looked up, her cheeks flushed, her eyes over-bright. 'Yes. Isn't it exciting? After all the things your father has said about young Mercier, imagine him coming to dinner at our house! I always thought that family way above us. They must be enormously rich. It seems incredible that Mr Mercier should even consider dining here. Do you think he can be thinking of promoting your father to some more important job? Why else should he come?'

Because he has designs on your daughter, thought Laura bitterly, but of course she dared not say such a thing. It would worry her mother too much. She had to lock this secret deep inside her, and rely on her own common sense as protection.

Aloud she said, 'Have you decided what to give him? I hope your plans aren't too elaborate. You know I'm only a moderate sort of cook, so you might as well forget any Cordon Bleu menu, Mother.'

Mrs Hallam sighed. 'I suppose so.' Her eyes slid furtively to Laura's face. 'Unless I cooked tonight...'

'No, Mother,' Laura said firmly. 'Out of the question. It would be too tiring for you.'

'What if I supervised?' Mrs Hallam begged. 'I could show you how to make something special. Oh, Laura, you know I love cooking, and it's so long since I spent any time in the kitchen!'

'I wish I could say yes,' Laura sighed. 'But Tom would never hear of it.'

'He needn't know!'

'And what if it made you ill? He'd find out then, and who would he blame?' Laura shook her head at her affectionately, her smile regretful. 'No, I'll do it on my own.'

'I could sit in the kitchen and watch,' her mother pleaded, green eyes wistful.

Laura hesitated, biting her lip. 'I suppose you could do that,' she agreed.

Mrs Hallam's eyes lit up. She swung her feet out of bed and was about to stand up when Laura said firmly, 'Oh, no, Mother! If you really want to stay in the kitchen while I cook you'll have to stay in bed this morning.'

Reluctantly Mrs Hallam got back into bed and Laura drew the covers over her, tidying her pillows and smoothing down the coverlet as she did so.

They discussed the menu for some time, then Laura left her mother reading a new library book and went downstairs to get the lunch under way. They were having a very simple meal and it did not take long. When she had finished, she went to the window to watch for Tom. He arrived after five minutes and ran up the path. She opened the door, smiling at him welcomingly.

Looking at his pale, tired face she felt an angry impulse of shame at the memory of those moments with Randal Mercier last night when she had been lost to everything but the passion of his lovemaking. Now the memory of those kisses seemed a momentary delusion. In front of her stood reality, her love for Tom unchanged.

'How is she this morning?' he asked, closing the door.

'Very cheerful,' Laura admitted. 'She's had some excitement, but I think she's coping with it quite well.'

Tom's brows drew together anxiously. 'What excitement?'

'Father's boss is coming to dinner tonight,' Laura told him.

Tom smiled. 'That's exciting?'

'Mother thinks so,' Laura smiled back.

His blue eyes frowned suddenly. 'She isn't planning to cook this dinner, I hope? I know what a fantastic cook she is, and how much she always loved cooking, but it would be far too much for her, Laura. You realise that, don't you?'

'I've told her as much very firmly,' she nodded. 'But I did promise to let her sit in the kitchen while I cook the meal.'

'Fatal!' he groaned. 'She won't be able to sit still for a second. I don't like this, Laura. She's so volatile. We can't have her exciting herself.'

She eyed him under her lashes, a sudden brilliant idea occurring to her. 'I know,' she said pleadingly. 'Why don't you come to dinner as well? Then you could keep an eye on her without her suspecting it.'

Tom gave her a thoughtful glance. 'It might be a good idea,' he admitted. 'But if this dinner is partly a business occasion I might be in the way.'

'It isn't really business,' she denied. 'Purely social—a return meal for the party last night. Do come, Tom. It will be rather boring for me otherwise.'

He laughed, his eyes indulgent. 'Minx! Very well, I'll

DISTURBING STRANGER   61

come, and thank you for the invitation. I'll go up and see your mother now. Has Doctor Ferguson seen her since yesterday?'

'No,' she said. 'He had to cancel his visit. He said he knew you would let him know if Mother's condition altered.' She smiled at him adoringly. 'He trusts you, Tom.'

Tom shrugged. 'He's a good doctor. Some men would object to my visits here, but Ferguson is bigger than that.'

'He knows you're one of the family,' she pointed out.

'Even so, some doctors would stand on medical etiquette. He never has.' Tom ran up the stairs and Laura went into the kitchen to make some coffee.

Later, as they sipped it together, she watched him as he talked about one of his patients, her eyes tracing the fine-boned strength of his tired face. He worked much too hard. He was running himself into the ground. He had little free time, but that never seemed to bother him. Utterly dedicated, he worked all out, often for half the night after a full day's work, and earned a much lower salary than he might have done had he gone into practice in some pleasant suburban area. He never bothered about his clothes—they were clean but shabby, and he needed some new shirts, she noticed. The one he was wearing was fraying at the cuffs. She would buy him a shirt for Christmas, she decided.

He stood up to go and she raised herself on tiptoe, saying teasingly, 'Your tie is crooked again ...' She straightened it, standing close to him, her eyes almost on a level with his for a moment. From this angle she could see the tiny yellow lines radiating from his irises and the rough graining of his skin.

He watched her unsmilingly. Suddenly she felt the tension which had sprung up between them. Her eyes widened revealingly, her lips parted on a sigh. Tom's face tightened as though he had received a blow. She heard his breath catch in his throat and then come faster.

Experimentally she leaned forward very slowly until her mouth touched his.

For a second he stood under her kiss without moving. Then he took hold of her shoulders and moved her away.

She flushed to her temples, trembling with shame. He had refused her kiss! She had made a fool of herself. She turned away, but Tom took her hand and held it warmly.

'Laurie,' he said huskily, 'don't look like that. Please, darling . . .'

Tears were pricking behind her lids. Her lips trembled. 'I'm sorry I embarrassed you,' she said flatly.

'You didn't embarrass me,' he repudiated at once. 'You know how fond I am of you. It was a delightful thing to do, but you mustn't do it again or I may lose my head.'

Her heart thudded. 'Perhaps I want you to lose your head,' she said shakily, smiling again.

'That wouldn't be very sensible,' he said roughly. He tried to laugh, his face very pale. 'My patients need a doctor with his head firmly screwed on!' He glanced at his watch. 'Which reminds me, time I was moving on. I've got a hundred things to do before tonight and you wouldn't want me to miss this fantastic dinner party, would you?'

She saw him to the door, angry with both him and herself for what had happened. She had exposed her feelings to him and he had rejected her. Confused, wounded, angry, she went on with the preparations for the dinner party, her mind far more occupied with Tom than with what she was doing. Even though he had quite definitely and unmistakably refused to follow up her kiss, she could not help believing he was not indifferent to her. His reaction was bewildering. Her instincts had told her he was giving her a positive reaction, yet on the surface he had been decidedly negative. Were her instincts at fault? Or was Tom himself confused?

When she told her father that evening that she had invited Tom, he was taken aback and looked at her irritably. 'What on earth did you do that for? That makes the numbers uneven. If you had to ask him you should have asked that lady friend of his, the social worker with the plain face.'

'I'm sorry, I didn't think of that,' she said, extremely glad she had not invited Pat. 'It's too late now. I don't suppose Mr Mercier will mind.'

Her father looked at her oddly, but said nothing. He had bought some wine for the party and was busy fussing over the correct temperature at which to serve it, so she escaped to her room to change.

She expected Tom to be the first arrival, but to her surprise Randal was there before him. When the door bell rang she skipped lightly along the hall, her spirits high, expecting to find Tom on the doorstep. Opening the door, her smile brilliant, she stared at the tall, dark man leaning negligently there, and her face dropped visibly.

'Oh, it's you,' she said without enthusiasm.

He raised his thin brows. 'Who did you expect?' The grey eyes surveyed her keenly.

She flushed. 'A friend of mine is joining us for dinner,' she explained.

She had an extraordinary feeling as she said the words, as if she had somehow switched on an electric current in him. The surge of power almost seemed to hum audibly. Her eyes opened wide and she stared at him.

He looked just the same, his handsome face lazily ironic, his smile casual. But she still received this impression of hidden menace.

From behind his back he produced a huge silver basket of dark red roses. 'For my hostess,' he drawled.

'Mother will be thrilled,' she said in astonishment, staring at the beautiful things.

His eyes narrowed. 'I meant you,' he said succinctly.

'Oh.' Laura blushed. 'Thank you,' she mumbled, carrying them through into the sitting-room. Her parents were not yet downstairs. James Hallam had been unable to decide which suit to wear and halfway through putting on one had changed his mind and taken it off.

She placed the basket of roses in a corner of the room where they glowed darkly with a rich damask sweetness which seemed to fill the room with overpowering perfume, particularly once the warmth of the room had brought out their heady scent.

'My parents won't be a minute,' she said shyly, unable to look at him without remembering their last meeting.

A long mirror hung on the wall behind her. Randal's eyes switched to her pale, floating reflection, her silvery hair, curled in tiny strings of plaits, giving her an almost barbaric splendour which somehow altered her usual appearance. Her dress was an old one; white muslin over pink taffeta. Originally it had been a bridesmaid's dress, and she had altered it herself, giving it a new scooped neckline and a wide pink satin sash which emphasised her tiny waist. Around her throat she wore a single string of small pink pearls.

Uneasy under his long scrutiny she plucked nervously at the pearls, pulling the rather ramshackle clasp undone. The necklace slid away down into her bodice.

Scarlet now, she hesitated, not knowing what to do. Randal gave a soft chuckle.

'Need some help?'

Before she knew his intention he had moved towards her, his slim fingers deftly retrieving the end of the necklace. Laura would have fled if her legs would have carried her, but for some reason her knees seemed on the point of buckling.

She ventured a glance upwards at his face, her gilt-tipped lashes flickering. He was smiling that tormenting, quizzical smile of his and prolonging quite deliberately the business of re-fastening the clasp, his hands fiddling at the back of her neck while he stood in front of her, looking down.

Suddenly the bell rang sharply and she jumped. Randal stood back, watching her, as she turned and ran to the front door. This time it was Tom, flushed and unusually tidy in his best suit, a dark one.

He looked down at her as he entered. 'You look enchanting, darling,' he said on a husky note, bending to kiss her cheek.

Her hands went up to clasp his shoulders, longing to prolong that rare expression of affection.

But he moved back immediately and glanced through the open door into the sitting-room. Randal stood opposite the door, his keen grey eyes observing them minutely. He was also wearing a dark suit, but the cut and style of his made manifest the difference in price between the two. Randal's tailor had cause to be proud of his product. It was superbly styled and superbly worn. Beside him Tom looked shabby and careworn. But it was at Tom that Laura looked with adoring tenderness as she carefully brought him a glass of sherry. When she had poured a glass for Randal she handed it to him with a brief cold smile.

'So you work in the East End?' Randal asked Tom, having been introduced. 'That must be exhausting.'

Tom shrugged. 'The job needs doing.'

'Do you work there because you have no choice, or did you choose the district?'

'I chose it,' Tom answered calmly.

Laura wound her hand through the crook of his arm and leaned on him with childlike intimacy, her green eyes shining up at him. 'Tom isn't in medicine for the money,' she said eagerly. 'He has a strong vocation.'

Tom glanced down at her tenderly and put a scolding finger on the end of her slim nose. 'Don't put a halo on my head, Laurie. I just do my job.'

'He's the most popular doctor in that district for years,' she said, determined to make Randal see Tom as she did. 'Everyone says so!'

'Everyone meaning Pat Basset,' Tom said teasingly. 'Pat is biased in my favour, remember.'

Laura's face reflected the tinge of jealousy she felt at the name of the other girl who loved him. 'I don't just mean Pat Basset! The people I met there told me so too...'

Tom grinned at Randal. 'This girl would turn my head if I believed every word she said!'

Randal was watching her expressionlessly, his hard

mouth set in a straight line, his grey eyes flinty.

'Here we are at last!' James Hallam cried from the door, coming forward to greet Randal. His manner to Tom was far less effusive, and Laura was resentful on Tom's behalf as she saw the curt nod her father gave him.

While Randal was talking to her mother she slipped away to the kitchen to supervise the last details of the meal which she and Mrs Knight had cooked together. Mrs Knight was moving around the kitchen, humming. She winked at Laura when she came in.

'Everything's ready, so don't fret. Shall we bring it through?' Pointing to the hostess trolley which stood in the middle of the room. Laura hastily inspected its contents and smiled with relief.

'That's great, Mrs Knight. Yes, bring it through.'

She returned to the sitting-room, her long skirts flying around her as she moved. Randal's grey eyes slid to watch her, but when she looked at Tom he was talking to her mother.

'The dinner is ready,' she said to the little group generally. 'Shall we go through?'

James Hallam presented an arm to his wife, grinning in mock gallantry.

Somehow Laura found herself walking beside Randal, but how it came about she was never quite sure, nor did she know how she came to be sitting beside him at the table with her father on her left side instead of Tom, as she had intended.

Glancing across the oval table, she shrugged her regret to Tom, who grinned at her and then turned to smile at Mrs Knight as she placed his diced melon in front of him. Laura had decided on a cold first course to make it easier on herself.

Spooning tiny, ice-cold portions of melon into her mouth, she listened as her father talked to Randal across her. Deftly Randal brought Mrs Hallam into the conversation, sliding out of it himself to ask Laura sotto voce if she had cooked the meal tonight.

'Yes,' she admitted. 'With Mrs Knight's help.'

He took another spoonful of melon, then asked her suddenly, 'Have you known Dr Nicol long?'

She was caught off guard, her eyes very revealing as she looked round at him. 'All my life,' she said, her voice faintly uneven.

'Really? So he's a sort of big brother to you?'

'No!' she snapped, her eyes widening further. 'Not at all.'

His mouth tightened into a thin, hard line. 'Why didn't you tell me you were in love with someone?' he drawled icily.

Her cheeks flamed and her eyes dropped away. Somehow he had succeeded again in knocking her off balance. Her heart was beating so fast she was astonished the rest of the table did not hear it. She had a strange miserable feeling in the pit of her stomach, as though she wanted to cry, although she could not imagine why.

When she looked up, Randal was talking to her mother across the table, his face charming, his smile persuasive.

The second course, braised chicken breasts rolled around liver paté, was served while she was still trying to recapture her earlier mood of gaiety. She brooded over her plate, barely speaking, and only surfaced when she found herself eating the sweet—a melting coffee cream laced with rum.

'I congratulate the chef,' Randal drawled, turning towards her for the first time since they were eating their melon.

She met his eyes nervously. They were cool and expressionless. He looked suddenly remote, a handsome unapproachable stranger. She felt a bitter sense of loss, although it was a ridiculous way to feel when she had never liked him anyway.

Mrs Knight wheeled away the hostess trolley to do the washing up while Laura moved around the sitting-room filling coffee cups. Everyone took a second cup and she retreated to the kitchen to make some more coffee.

Tom followed her out there and leaned on the wall talking to her lightly. The fragrance of coffee filled the room. She took the cream out of the refrigerator and poured some into the cream jug, smiling at Tom as she did so. 'Put this on the tray for me,' she asked, handing it to him.

He obeyed and she turned to switch off the coffee. Turning away towards him, she collided with him. They laughed, their bodies touching, their arms around each other as he supported her so that she would not fall.

Laura's green eyes shone as she looked up at him. 'Oh, Tom,' she murmured huskily, 'did you mean what you said this morning? Do I really make you lose your head?'

His face sobered rapidly. He looked anxious and disturbed. 'I shouldn't have said any such thing,' he told her. 'Forget it.'

'How can I?' The cry was charged with pain. 'I don't understand, Tom. Sometimes I think ...' She broke off, suddenly seeing the sharp-etched outline of a listening shape on the wall of the hall. Randal was out there, silently eavesdropping. As if he sensed that she had seen him he pushed open the door and came into the room.

Tom's arms dropped away from her. He was flushed and unhappy. 'I'll take the tray in,' he said, picking it up and moving out of the room.

Mrs Knight had gone. She was alone with Randal. She gave him a resentful look. He had interrupted her brief moments with Tom, and she hated him for it.

She had prepared some thin slices of orange and lemon to serve with the coffee. She got them out and busily arranged them on a glass plate. Randal watched her, leaning easily on the back of a chair, his dark face brooding.

'Do I get the impression that the path of true love does not run smoothly?' he drawled suddenly.

His suggestion brought a prick of pain and she turned on him at once. 'Why must you sneer?'

He shrugged. 'I find it a surprising match—a girl of your spirit, with the eyes of a wildcat and the temper of a tigress, and a young man with such an austere, controlled face. I can only imagine he finds your ardent attentions difficult to resist.' The grey eyes insolently surveyed her, lingering on the white curve of her half-revealed breasts. 'You're a tempting little creature to any man.'

She felt her face burn and that betraying pulse began to beat at her wrists and the base of her long, white throat.

'You have no right to say such things to me,' she said tamely, and hated him for laughing.

'I thought you were more honest,' he murmured. 'You must curb this tendency to lapse into vulgar cliché. When we first met it amused me to hear you snap back with the bite of a fishwife. It was such an odd contrast to your appearance.'

She could not help looking at him enquiringly, her vanity aroused by the last remark, and suddenly something sparked in the cool grey eyes.

'You're a born coquette,' he said softly.

She lowered her gilt-tipped lashes and looked at him through them, her green eyes bright as glass. 'What a horrid thing to say!'

He moved with that startling rapidity, watching her with the intent gaze of a cat at a mousehole, and she felt her pulses stir into galloping life. Randal Mercier was a dangerous man, shrewd, practised in the art of flirtation, disguising his own thoughts and feelings but quick to read those of other people.

His hands took her by the shoulders and shook her. 'Behave yourself!' he said, but his tone was uneven. 'Do you even know what you're doing half the time? If you look at me like that, I warn you, I'll kiss you until your head spins.'

Her head was spinning now, she thought, half excited, half afraid. She was flirting with danger, but she could not resist another glance at him through her long fair lashes.

'You asked for this,' he said between his teeth as he bent towards her.

Without even knowing it her body curved towards him, her mouth eager. His lips were cruel, demanding ruthlessly her passionate response. If only Tom would kiss me like this, she thought, drowningly, her whole body on fire as she wound her arms around his neck.

Suddenly she was free and he was standing a foot away from her, his face cold. 'You were not kissing me.'

he said contemptuously. 'I won't be a stand-in for another man. Never try to use me like that again.'

She was instantly scarlet, her eyes like daggers as she looked back at him. Picking up the plate of fruit, she left him to bring the coffee and walked out of the room.

She poured coffee, then sat down to listen while her father talked to Randal. Her mother yawned and stood up, excusing herself. 'I'm afraid I have to go to bed early, but do stay and talk to my husband.'

Laura went upstairs with her to see her into bed. She was grateful for the chance to escape. When she returned downstairs it was to find Tom with his coat on just leaving. She looked at him with disappointment. She had hoped to see more of him this evening, but somehow it had not happened.

He kissed her and went out, closing the door with a snap. She went into the kitchen to wash up the coffee cups and was just putting them away when Randal put his head round the door.

'Goodnight, Miss Hallam,' he said distantly. 'It was a delightful meal.'

'I'm glad you enjoyed it,' she said, equally distant.

He hesitated, as if to add something, then thought better of it and went away. She heard the front door slam and then her father yawned himself into the kitchen. 'I'm off to bed, Laura,' he said.

'Goodnight, Dad,' she smiled.

He gave her a furtive little glance. 'Was it my imagination, or would you say our Mr Mercier is rather smitten with you?'

She flushed and looked angry. 'I'd say it was your imagination, Dad.'

He shrugged. 'Maybe.' Whistling, he went to bed.

DISTURBING STRANGER 73

Next morning Laura went out to do the shopping and take her short walk in the park. She carried a wicker basket in one hand and wore old blue jeans and a thick white polo-neck sweater. The weather was quite warm, although the trees were now totally denuded. She wandered down to the lake and threw some old bread to the ducks. While she stood there she heard a familiar step and turned to see Randal at her side, his hands in his pockets and a mocking tilt to his well-shaped head.

'What are you doing here?' she asked him crossly.

'Don't turn round,' he said softly. 'I was just admiring the purity of your profile. It has a clarity of outline which is enchanting.'

Laura felt like stamping her foot in a fit of childish rage. Instead she turned and walked away round the lake, watching the wind carry a skeletal leaf in twirling dance across the water.

He kept pace with her without effort, but made no attempt to speak to her, irritating her so much that at last she halted and faced him.

'What do you want?' she demanded.

'I could answer that in a monosyllable,' he drawled. 'But I won't—to spare your blushes, and particularly, to spare me any of your vulgar clichés.'

'Are you trying to make me angry?' she asked, her chin lifted scornfully.

His eyes suddenly twinkled. 'You do look very pretty when you're in a temper,' he admitted. 'But no—I came to ask you to come to the theatre tonight.'

'No, thank you,' she said promptly.

He ignored her reply. 'I've already spoken to your father,' he murmured. 'He was delighted to accept my invitation.'

Her heart sank. 'You ... you blackmailer!' she flung at him.

He laughed, his eyes dancing. 'There you go again, my sweet. More clichés!'

Laura turned back towards the gate, scowling. He strolled along beside her, keeping a space between them. When they came to her house he halted. She walked up the path without looking back at him. As she let herself in he called softly, 'I'll be here at seven. Be ready.'

She did not deign to answer, slamming the door behind her. But at seven she was in the sitting-room waiting when he rang the door bell. Her father, glowing proudly, met him and led him into the room. She stood up, her lower lip set sulkily.

'This is very kind of you,' James Hallam said fulsomely. 'Isn't it, Laura?'

'Very kind,' she said without meeting Randal's eyes. He held her white jacket for her as she slipped into it and then opened the front door for her. She walked past, nose in the air.

They drove to the West End and parked, walked through the brightly lit, busy streets to the theatre and took their seats. He had got tickets for a lively comedy, and Laura could not maintain her pose of offended irritation for long. Soon she was laughing, her body warm and relaxed, already forgetting her anger. It was a rare pleasure for her to visit the theatre. She could not refuse to enjoy herself.

They had a drink in the bar in the interval. Laura was thirsty, so had a long cold lemonade, the chunks of ice tinkling as she sipped it.

'Each time I see you, I see a different girl,' Randal said with a faint smile. 'This morning you were boyish in your jeans. Last night you were a glittering princess. Tonight you look like a little girl.'

She had deliberately chosen a dress which made her look very young—a simple grey woollen pinafore with a pink sweater worn under it—giving her the appearance of a schoolgirl.

Leaning over to whisper in her ear, he asked, 'Do you feel like a little girl tonight?' The question was somehow tantalising and made her blush angrily.

The bell went and they returned to their seats. In the warm darkness his hand found hers and captured it. She wriggled, trying to free her fingers, but his grip was too strong, and without making a scene she had to leave her hand in his possession. As her hand relaxed, abandoning the struggle, he lifted it to his mouth discreetly and kissed her wrist, finding the fast-beating pulse which quickened at the touch of his mouth. She ignored what he was doing, fastening her attention on the stage, but he was unashamedly proceeding from one liberty to another, his mouth slowly crawling over her palm, her fingers, kissing them with seductive care.

She lifted her foot until her sharp stiletto heel was directly over his shoe, then stamped down hard. The only sign he gave was a sharp intake of breath. Then he laughed softly and lowered her hand, still retaining it a captive on his lap.

When the lights finally came up, they made their way out of the theatre. Randal suggested having supper before they went home, but she icily refused, so they walked back to the car and drove to her house.

She dived for the door as he drew up outside, but he was too quick for her, his hand grabbing her round the waist and hauling her back against his shoulder.

'Let me go, you brute!' she hissed, striking at him with a clenched fist.

'Not just yet, Little Tommy Tucker,' he drawled. 'You have to sing for your supper first, or I should say theatre ticket.'

She looked at him scornfully. 'I suspected you were that sort of man!'

'Nice to have your suspicions confirmed,' he murmured, bending her back until his mouth was poised over hers.

She felt her head swimming as she looked up at his dark, inverted face. All the struggle went out of her and she met his descending mouth with a reckless blazing passion that made his body tighten and his arms close round her like vices. Tumultuous seas seemed to crash over Laura's head, sweeping her away into waters she had never ventured into before, tossing her high into the air and pulling her down again to drown helplessly. She heard herself gasping, her hands clenched against his chest in an effort to push him away, but the long kiss quickened again and her hands uncurled and moved up his shirt. She twirled a finger aimlessly around one of his buttons while the kiss blazed on, then, as he drew away at last to take a long, gasping breath, found her finger slipping inside his shirt to touch his naked warm flesh.

The discovery went to her head. She undid another button and another, her hands restlessly touching him and fluttering away like small white moths which could neither settle nor fly away.

Randal watched her in the darkness, his eyes glittering. After a moment he began to kiss her throat, his lips seductive as they softly caressed her. When those seductive lips reached the soft warm swelling of her breasts she made a moaning sound, pushing one hand at his head to deny him.

He captured her hand and returned it firmly to his chest, splaying her fingers against his skin, then bent his head once more and this time when his mouth poached on the forbidden territory she made no protest, totally engrossed in her own discovery about the hard-muscled wall of his chest which had a masculine excitement she had never experienced before.

Suddenly Randal raised his head. 'I think now is where we stop,' he said thickly.

Laura had just realised that she wanted to rest her hot face against him, bury herself in the security of his body. She was dazed as she looked at him, her eyes feverish.

'Randal,' she breathed, as if his name was unfamiliar. Flopping like a rag doll, she lay against him, her mouth against his skin, her lips parted and opening to kiss his chest.

He lifted her up by the shoulders and pushed her back into her own seat. His breathing was harsh in the enclosed space of the car.

'What would the Beloved Physician say if he saw you now?' he asked cruelly.

For a second she was totally still, then she gave a little, agonised cry, like the mew of a kitten in torment, and dived out of the car to run up the path and let herself into the house.

Her back against the door, breathing hard, tears running down her face, she shook with self-contempt and misery.

She had totally betrayed her love for Tom. She had betrayed her own self-respect. Her life lay in ruins around her as she realised just how close she had come to offering herself to a man whom she hated and despised.

There was a traitor in her body, a dangerous enemy who emerged when she least expected it, leading her down a path of fatal enchantment. What sort of girl was she? she asked herself in despair. How could she have behaved in that disgusting fashion with him? The burning, fevered abandonment of the senses which Randal seemed capable of awaking in her had nothing to do with love. It was something with a much uglier name, and she seemed unable to resist it. How could she fight Randal when her own body was his ally? Her mind and heart rejected him, but each time battle was joined he only had to arouse her sleeping passion to win hands down.

'I hate him,' she whispered into the deaf silence. 'I hate him, and I hate myself ...'

CHAPTER FIVE

SHE did not see Randal again for a week. Then one evening he drove her father home from the office, bringing a basket of purple-bloomed hothouse grapes for her mother. Laura was in the kitchen cooking dinner. Her heart thudded when she heard his voice in the hall, but he did not come into the kitchen until after he had sat talking to her parents for ten minutes. Carrying the silver basket of grapes, he appeared in the doorway at last, his expression giving nothing away.

She looked up, her face flushed and hostile.

Randal gave her a casual nod, placed the basket on the table and sampled a piece of her home-made shortbread, which was lying on a plate there.

'Are you staying to dinner?' she asked brusquely.

'Are you inviting me?' he asked in return.

'My father hasn't?'

He shook his head.

She moved away to stir the cream of onion soup simmering on the hob. He leaned back in a chair and watched silently as she went on working. Laura was angrily aware of him every second of the time, but she ignored him.

After a while he got up and left without a word, leaving her puzzled and confused.

Was his pursuit of her over? she wondered, as day after day passed by and he did not come to the house. She told herself she was relieved, but she knew she was lying to herself. Beneath the surface of her mind lay a sense of loss which she did not understand. She hated him, so why should she miss him?

Tom's visits had, of course, continued, but she could not suppress a feeling of anguished guilt whenever she saw him. He did not know how her body had betrayed her heart, but she felt as if it must be written on her face every time they met. She could hardly believe he could not see it.

A few days after her twentieth birthday party Randal arrived before lunch with a pile of paperbacks for her mother. Mrs Hallam was astonished and delighted. He sat talking to her until Laura was finally forced to invite him to lunch. It infuriated her that he then refused with a cool smile and left.

Over dinner that evening James Hallam said genially, 'Our Mr Mercier is becoming quite a fixture in this house, I gather, Laura. I wonder what the attraction can be?' His teasing smile brought an angry blush to her face, which only confirmed her parents' suspicions.

Autumn passed imperceptibly into winter. Life in the Hallam household moved to its established pattern, but Randal Mercier was gradually becoming an accepted part of that pattern. Laura saw him so often, sometimes so briefly, that she gradually ceased to regard him as a threat, and became accustomed to his presence around the house, forgetting the danger he still represented—rather as one might grow used to having an unexploded bomb in one's garden for years, treating it casually without considering its potential.

He dined with them occasionally, but more often he merely came during the day and sat in the kitchen watching her work, or walked with her to the shops to carry her basket. The first tension between them eased day by day to a quiet familiarity. Some evenings he arrived after dinner and played Scrabble or draughts with her. Once he had tickets for the theatre. Another time he drove her and her mother to see a firework display on Bonfire Night.

Never once during all this time did he attempt to make love to her. If their hands brushed while they played Scrabble she would flush, but Randal seemed unaware of the brief contact.

One evening in December her father came home pale and tense. Laura was concerned, but when she questioned him he brushed aside her questions irritably. At this time of the year the firm always had its audit, so she presumed he was suffering the effect of overwork.

The following evening after dinner he suddenly announced that Randal would be there at any moment. Glancing at his watch, he said, 'He said he would be here at nine.'

Laura nodded casually, winding silk for her mother, her hands and mind busy.

'He ... he has something he wants to ask you,' her father added with a nervous stammer.

She looked up, then, a premonition sending her pulses leaping.

Before she could question her father, Randal was ringing the door bell. Mr Hallam jumped up to answer it, and showed him into the room, then withdrew, taking his wife with him, giving Laura a last anxious look as he closed the door.

Randal stood looking at her, his grey eyes darkly intent. She felt her heart begin to thud apprehensively. A strange tremor ran along her nerves.

When he spoke it was in a tone so remote and expressionless that for a moment she did not believe what she heard. 'Will you marry me?'

She stared at him, trying to make sense of the words. Was he serious? But why ask at all if he cared so little what her reply might be? Beneath her bewilderment ran a sharp pang of triumph. She could not silence the realisation that Randal Mercier must want her very badly if he was prepared to marry her. It was shameful for such a thought to please her, but her feminine instincts were too strong for her to resist it.

He had warned her that he always got what he wanted. He had proved already that he was ruthless in his pursuit of his desire. She had made it clear that she would never be his mistress, so now he was determined to make her his wife in order to achieve his ends.

Yet she was still puzzled. His eyes were fixed on her face, their colour darkened by the intensity of his gaze. He was very pale. The skin was drawn tight across his cheekbones, his lips pressed together, as though in pain or anger. Was his proposal ironic? Was it a bitter joke?

'I would like an answer,' he said coolly when she made no reply. 'I realise this has taken you by surprise ...'

'You know what my answer will be,' she said flatly. 'You know I love Tom—I've never pretended otherwise. I'm flattered by your proposal, but I must refuse.'

Calmly, as if he had not heard, he went on, 'Speak to your father. I'll come back tomorrow for my reply.'

Her dignity dissolved in a wave of rage more violent than any he had aroused in her before. 'Don't you understand English? I don't want to marry you. I don't love you!'

He walked to the door. She ran after him and caught

DISTURBING STRANGER

at his arm, furious that he should turn his back on her, leaving her in such a turmoil of anger and confusion.

He turned and looked down at her, his mouth rigid. Looking at his icily controlled face, Laura found it hard to believe that this was the man who had once made passionate love to her and carried her away on a flood-tide of passion.

'I mean what I say!' she told him fiercely. 'I would die rather than marry you!'

He gently removed her hand from his arm. 'My dear, events have moved too fast. You must marry me,' he said flatly.

Then he had gone, closing the door after him. Laura stared in complete bewilderment. What did he mean?

A moment later the door opened and her father hurried into the room, his face worried as he looked at her. 'Why has he left? What happened?' he demanded.

She could see that her father had known the purpose of Randal's visit, so she said bluntly, 'I refused him.'

'Refused him?' James Hallam repeated the words as if he did not comprehend them. Slowly all the colour drained out of his face. He swayed on his feet. 'Oh, my God,' he groaned. 'You've ruined me!'

She was taken aback by the violence of his reaction. She had suspected he would want her to marry Randal Mercier. After all, it was a wonderful chance for her. But this was more than mere disappointment. Her father showed signs of positive shock.

He sat down in a chair heavily, dropping his head into his hands.

She knelt beside his chair, her small face anxious. 'Dad, what's wrong? What is it?'

'I've been embezzling money from the firm for years,'

he said thickly, 'and Randal Mercier has found out.'

'Oh, no!' she moaned, turning white.

'How do you think I've managed to keep you and your mother in comfort all these years? I never earned the sort of money I needed. It was a temptation ... handling vast sums of money while I only earned a pittance ... when your mother started to have her attacks I had to have money for private treatment, delicacies, little treats ... I love her, Laura. I couldn't bear to see her go without anything ...' He raised his head, breathing hard. 'Don't blame me too much.'

She was trying to understand what had happened. 'You say Randal knows?'

He nodded, his eyes sick. 'He's suspected for a long time—I knew that. But I was always so careful. I'm a damned good accountant. I juggled the books too well for anything to be traced. Then he started coming here so often and I could see ...' He broke off, swallowing. 'I realised he was attracted to you, and I thought everything was going to work out all right. Then I suppose I relaxed for the first time for years, and I got careless. I made a mistake. And when they ran the audit they found it ... and others ... once they really started digging it all came out.'

Laura closed her eyes in horror. 'What did he say?'

James Hallam ran a dry tongue over his lips. 'Don't ask me that. After he'd told me what he thought of me, he dropped his bombshell. I was standing there feeling sick waiting for the police to arrive, when he suddenly said he wouldn't proceed against me because he intended to marry you and he didn't want any scandal in the family.'

'Oh, God!' she whispered, white as paper. 'So that was it.'

Her father looked at her pleadingly. 'You like him, don't you? He's a handsome swine. Other women seem to fall for him like ninepins. Why on earth can't you do the same, Laura? You'd be rich and safe. He's generous to his family. You would never want for anything.'

'I love Tom,' she cried in anguish.

Her father's face reflected his irritation. 'Tom Nicol? A stubborn, poverty-stricken slum doctor? You can't compare the two. Mercier would shower you with money. All Nicol can offer you is a life of struggle.'

'A life without love,' she said dryly. 'Is that what you want for me, Dad?'

He looked angry for a moment, then his anger fell away like a cloak and he said miserably, 'If you won't do it for yourself, do it for me and your mother.'

She stared, her eyes wide and shaken. 'You think he'll prosecute you if I refuse to marry him? Surely he couldn't be so ruthless! Even he wouldn't do that.'

He shrugged. 'I'm not so sure. But even if he doesn't call the police, I'm finished—he made that clear. I couldn't work at the firm again, and who else would take me on? Mercier wouldn't give me a reference, and I can't blame him for that. So where in God's name do I find work at my age without a reference? It would be obvious to everyone that there must be a reason why the firm refused me a reference after so many years' service. I wouldn't have a snowball's chance in hell of getting another job.'

Laura was trembling now, her hands and feet icy cold with shock. 'Oh, Dad, what are we going to do?'

'Laura,' he said pleadingly. 'Your mother ... that's all

I care about now. She must never know. It would literally kill her—you know the doctors have said another shock would do it. I wouldn't ask you for myself, I could manage somehow. But your mother ... what about her?'

She wanted to cry, but somehow she fought back the stinging tears. 'I've no real choice, have I?' She remembered Randal's last words. A bitter, ironic smile curved her pale lips. 'He knew that. Damn him!'

Eagerly, James Hallam said, 'I'm certain he would do all he could to make you happy, darling. He wouldn't want to marry you if he didn't genuinely care for you.'

Oh, wouldn't he? she thought savagely. Her father had no idea. He did not know about Randal's long, amoral pursuit of her. He didn't understand the complex nature of the man he worked for, or realise the depth of his determination to have his own way.

She stood up, squaring her shoulders as if to face a dark future.

Her father looked at her with sick hope in his eyes. 'What are you going to do?'

'What do you think?' she asked him. 'I'll have to marry him.'

How was she to tell Tom? she asked herself desperately as she worked in the house next morning. This was going to come as a terrible shock to him. She was sure he had never suspected that Randal might want to marry her.

When he rang the bell half an hour later she went to let him in, her green eyes enormous in her white face. Tom looked at her in alarmed concern.

'What's wrong? Your mother?' His eyes shot up the stairs. 'Is she worse?'

'No,' she shook her head. 'Come into the kitchen, Tom. I must talk to you.'

He followed her anxiously. Laura stood straight, like a child caught out in a misdeed, her hands tightly clenched at her waist, and faced him.

'Randal Mercier has asked me to marry him,' she said huskily.

She saw the shock in Tom's eyes. Then abruptly he turned away and walked to the window, turning his back to her.

She watched his back painfully. 'I refused at first,' she said slowly. 'But then my father told me something that makes it plain I have no choice but to accept.'

Tom swung round at that, frowning. 'What do you mean?'

'Dad ... Dad is in financial difficulties. We need Randal's money.' It was as far as she could go. She dared not tell him the whole truth; she had no right to. But she could not bear Tom to think she was marrying Randal because she loved him.

There was a long pause. She listened to the sound of Tom's slow breathing. All her life lay in the hollow of his hand. Her eyes traced the slight stoop of his shoulders, the lift of his neck, the shape of the skull beneath his sunny hair. The light falling through the window showed her a few white hairs among the gold. He's past thirty, she thought. He'll be middle-aged in a few years. Her heart ached with tenderness. She had loved him all her life, hurrying to grow up so that she could marry him, and the thought of a future without him was bitter.

He sighed and gave her a smile, a pale, cold movement of his mouth which did not reach his eyes.

'What will you do?' he asked her.

'As my father wishes,' she answered in a tone as calm as his own, betraying nothing of the pain which was twisting deep inside her like a snake of poison.

If only he would show some sign of regret or sorrow, give her some comfort to take with her into the darkness of the future. Her eyes searched his face. A pulse at his temple, the only clue to any emotion.

He flushed under her scrutiny. 'Are you sure there's no other way?' he asked abruptly. 'If you're unwilling to marry him, we might find a way to help your father ...'.

She shook her head. 'No, it's impossible. I can't tell you ... I've no right to tell you ... but I have no choice, Tom.'

He nodded quietly. 'At least you'll always be cherished and protected,' he said, half to himself. 'You'll never go without or be lonely. He'll wrap you in cotton wool.' His eyes rested on her face. 'You're so small and fragile, darling. He's the sort of man you need to take care of you ...'

You are the man I need, her heart cried out, but Tom was deaf to her heart and quietly walked out of the room, closing the door. Laura went to the window and stared out at the grey winter sky for a moment, then she went on with her work, moving carefully, as one moves when every step means a stab of agony.

Randal came later that afternoon. She opened the door to him and he walked quietly past her, wearing a stylish dark suit which gave him a sombre magnificence.

She looked at him and felt nothing. She seemed to exist in another world, removed from feeling of any kind, frozen in the realisation that she would never now belong to Tom.

'I've come for my answer,' he said. The grey eyes observed with cool penetration. His mouth closed in a thin line as he waited for her answer.

'I will marry you,' she said. The words were easy to speak now. They meant nothing: she had achieved that much at least. There was some comfort in being remote, placed above the pain which had first begun to throb yesterday. It had been a long battle, but she had fought her way through it to a quiet place.

He started at her in silence for a moment, then with a savage gesture he caught her by her shoulders, staring down into her white face. 'You look like one of the walking dead,' he said.

Laura felt a prick of irritation. She felt as though, having written a scene for him to play, he had refused to follow the words. Dislike for him filled her wide green eyes. It was typical of him! From their first meeting he had been jabbing and prodding at her, making her respond in ways which had horrified and astonished her.

'What do you expect? I'm hardly a joyful bride. You've got your way—I'm going to marry you. Don't expect me to dance with delight as well.'

Randal's mouth compressed. 'Have you told the Beloved Physician?'

Her eyes threw contempt at him. 'Yes,' she said shortly.

His lips twisted savagely. 'Didn't he try to talk you out of it, this passionate lover of yours?'

'He isn't my lover!' she cried in anguish.

'But how you wish he were,' he taunted.

'I've never hidden my feelings from you,' she snapped.

'Or from him,' he drawled with a sneer. 'But he's never

responded, has he, my sweet? There's no red blood in his veins.'

'What makes you so certain of that?' she asked, lowering her lashes to disguise her expression.

'Your response to me,' he said bitingly. 'If the noble doctor had been more passionate you would have slapped my face, but you were half mad with frustration, weren't you, my sweet?' His hands ran down her body, caressing her.

'You don't love me, do you?' she cried angrily. 'Why do you want to marry me?'

His hands had found the buttons on her blouse. He slowly undid them one by one, bending his dark head to kiss her creamy skin. His mouth open against her, he whispered, 'I don't want your stupid sentimental little heart, my dear, I want your body. As marriage is the only way I'm ever going to get it, I'll marry you.'

She pulled his head back, her fingers tangled in his hair. He smiled at her cruelly, seizing her shoulders again. They stood struggling for a moment, then he bent her slowly backwards and kissed her, his lips slow and hot on hers, seducing her into a response she could neither control nor disguise.

When at last he raised his head she was trembling, her body so weak she would have fallen had he not held her. Her eyes looked at him, hating him almost to the point of frenzy.

'The Beloved Physician has never kissed you like that,' he said thickly. 'Leave your heart with him if you like, but I'll have no ghosts in my bed, my sweet. When I make love to you I want to be sure you aren't thinking of another man.'

'I don't know why you're bothering to marry me,' she

said with scornful bitterness. 'You're in a position to dictate terms. You could have me without any wedding ceremony now.'

His grey eyes danced wickedly. 'Could I, Laura? Is this a firm proposition?'

She took a shaky breath. 'If you like,' she whispered.

'And when do I take delivery?' he asked tormentingly. 'Tonight? It would certainly solve the problem of waiting ...'

White, trembling, she said uncertainly, 'You ... mean you would accept the idea?'

His face changed, grew cool. 'No, my dear,' he said firmly. 'No. I'm afraid the arrangement, although tempting, would not do. You see, I don't think the temporary nature of the liaison would be sufficient for me.' His grey eyes ran down lingeringly over her body. 'I don't think I shall tire of you very quickly. You're far too lovely.'

She flushed hotly, while a wave of sick relief swept over her. She had made the suggestion to insult him but when he appeared to take it seriously she had been terrified.

He grinned, watching her. 'I think I should warn you, I can read every expression on that face of yours. I may never own your heart, but your mind already belongs to me, and soon I'll own your body, too.'

'You don't own my mind,' she flung bitterly.

'Let's say I understand it, then,' he suggested coolly. 'You will not, I hope, dispute my ownership of your body?'

Her face was scarlet. 'You have all the attitudes of a slave master!'

Randal grinned again. 'I certainly intend to be the

master of your body,' he agreed shamelessly. 'I intended it from our first meeting. One look at you and I knew I had to have you. You're not only very beautiful, Laura, you're a sensual and exciting creature. You won't believe me now, but I assure you, our marriage is going to be a satisfying experience for both of us.'

She looked at him with hatred.

He smiled derisively. 'No comeback? Good.' He looked at his watch. 'Is it possible for you to come out with me now to choose your ring?'

She was bewildered. 'My ring?'

'You'll need an engagement ring,' he pointed out, smiling.

Mrs Knight was upstairs with her mother, watching a film on the television in her mother's bedroom. Mrs Hallam had a slight cold and Tom had suggested she stay in bed all day until it was better.

Laura ran up to tell her mother she was going out, then joined Randal in his long, sleek car. They drove to a famous London jeweller's and were shown a wide selection of engagement rings. Laura was dazzled by them. She had no idea which to choose. Randal picked up a large square-cut emerald set in diamonds.

'I prefer this one,' he said, slipping it on her finger.

The jeweller looked blandly satisfied.

Laura felt the beautiful ring heavy on her slender finger. It was a badge of ownership, a modern version of the slave ring, and she hated it. But she said politely that it was very beautiful, and Randal nodded at the jeweller.

'We'll take it,' he said, removing it from her finger.

The jeweller found a box for it and when they had paid the bill with a cheque Randal drove her home. In the sitting-room they confronted each other like enemies.

He took her hand, raising it, and slid the ring slowly on to her finger. For a moment they both stared at the green blaze against her white skin.

Randal bent his dark head and kissed her hand, his lips warm and lingering.

'You're mine,' he said as he straightened, and Laura heard the unmistakable ring of triumph in his voice.

Her eyes were full of angry bitterness as she watched him. He looked into her face and read her expression, and the smile vanished from his mouth.

A small muscle twitched in his lean cheek. The long mouth grew hard, taut, reined in by anger or contempt. Suddenly Laura wondered if he were as sure of himself as he pretended to be.

She lowered her lashes, watching him through them secretly. The grey eyes watched her back, then his mouth softened into a mocking smile.

'Are you flirting with me, Laura?' he asked softly.

Excitement was pounding in her veins. She did not know or understand herself at all. She only knew she wanted to see that blazing look of passion in his face, the look she was beginning to recognise.

At that moment Mrs Knight tapped on the door, startling them. She came in to say she was leaving, giving Randal a look of curious interest.

When she had gone again, Randal moved towards the door. Laura watched him in surprise. He turned and said calmly, 'I think it's time you met my family. I'll get my mother to arrange something. Goodnight, Laura.'

'Goodnight,' she answered blankly. When he had gone she stood staring at nothing, wondering why she felt flat and drained.

CHAPTER SIX

THE engagement puzzled Mrs Hallam. She had known for so long that her daughter loved Tom Nicol. How was she to take this sudden decision to marry another man? Of course Randal's frequent visits, and her husband's elephantine hints, had prepared her mind to some extent. It had been blatantly obvious to her that Randal Mercier was very attracted to her daughter. She had even suspected that Laura was not unresponsive to him. Even so, she had not expected her to marry him.

Anxious, bewildered, she waited for a chance to talk to Laura alone, hoping to discover the truth from her. But Laura was suddenly evasive, always in a hurry, always unwilling to discuss anything more serious than the menu for the next meal. Her very evasion made her mother more worried than ever. Why would Laura not talk to her? There had to be some reason.

At last she caught Laura alone for a while, and Laura was too spent to flee her mother's questions any longer.

'Darling, are you sure you know what you're doing?' Mrs Hallam asked her, taking her hands between her own.

Laura lay back in her chair, her eyes weary. 'Quite sure, Mother.'

'Do you love him?'

The question was not unexpected, but it threw Laura off balance. Hot colour ran up from her neck and covered her face. She looked down, her lips trembling.

Trying to answer lightly, she said, 'Why else would I marry a man, Mother?'

'You might be tempted by all his money,' Mrs Hallam told her quietly. 'Are you, Laura?'

Laura laughed almost feverishly. 'Not a bit, I promise you!'

Mrs Hallam gave a little sigh. 'I hope you're telling me the truth. It would be tragic if you found you weren't suited to each other after all...'

Randal came in quietly as she was speaking. His voice made Mrs Hallam jump.

'We're perfectly suited to each other, Mrs Hallam. You don't need to worry.'

Laura's eyes flew up to his face and her whole body gave a convulsive shudder. Her mother felt it and looked at her daughter quickly.

Randal strolled forward and bent to kiss Laura. Mrs Hallam watched as her daughter obediently lifted her face. The slender lines of the girl's body tautened as Randal's mouth touched hers, and one hand fluttered up to grasp his neck. Mrs Hallam looked away, suddenly embarrassed by the naked hunger with which the two kissed. All her doubts vanished. There was no doubt about anything any more. She was convinced that Laura was passionately in love. What else could such a scene mean?

'My mother has arranged for a family gathering next week,' Randal said huskily, moving away. He straightened his tie and smiled at Mrs Hallam. His face was darkly flushed and he was breathing fast.

'I hope you'll be fit enough to come, Mrs Hallam,' he added politely. 'My mother is looking forward to meeting you.'

'I shall be pleased to meet her,' she said with a shy smile. She watched him, admiring his hard good looks and assured bearing. Now that she was sure Laura was not marrying for money, she was delighted at the prospect of having such a son-in-law. Her husband had already hinted that he would be promoted soon. Her world was all sunshine for the moment.

'I've come to take Laura for a drive,' Randal said coolly, his eyes flickering to Laura's face.

'That will be nice,' said Mrs Hallam. 'Run along, dear. I'll be fine while Mrs Knight is with me.'

Laura rose and got ready, folding herself into a thick winter coat, a knitted white scarf tied round her head as a shawl.

As they drove out towards the countryside which surrounds London on all sides, Randal said coolly, 'Your mother seemed distressed. Is she very anxious about our marriage? I suppose she prefers the idea of a doctor son-in-law?'

'She knows I love Tom,' said Laura, not caring how she hit out at him.

He was silent for a while. He parked in a quiet layby and said calmly, 'We'll walk for a while. There's a footpath over there.'

The footpath wound across ploughed fields, beside the tangled hedgerows, leading them uphill at first, then plunging down to a village with a tapering church spire for a centre.

Randal paused on the hilltop, beneath some bare elms, and said quietly, 'Are you anxious about meeting my family?'

'A little,' she admitted.

'You needn't be,' he said, leaning on a stile, his brooding gaze on her face. 'They're delighted with the engagement.'

'They don't even know me,' she protested.

'They've been nagging me to get married for years,' he said with a shrug. 'My father is obsessed with the idea of grandsons. He would worship you if you gave him one.'

Laura felt her cheeks burn and turned to stare across the dreaming grey landscape. Far away the horizon was misty, opalescent. There were some cows grazing in a pasture nearby and a row of magpies sitting on a fence watching them curiously.

'Is that really why you want to marry?' she asked. 'To have children?'

'Partly,' he admitted coolly. 'I've already told you my other reason.'

'I'm sure you could find other girls as pretty as me,' she protested softly. 'Girls who would be eager to give you what you want without marriage.'

He moved behind her, his hands invading her beneath her thick coat, running over her body from breast to hip, pulling her back to rest against him while his mouth explored the softness of her neck and nuzzled below the silken strands of her silvery hair.

'I won't pretend there aren't always girls available to satisfy any masculine need,' he murmured lightly. 'I happen to want you.'

'Why me?' she asked with a curious sensation of breathlessness.

He laughed mockingly. 'Don't you know? Your body excites me to the point of frenzy.'

She began to tremble, putting up her hands to push his too-intrusive fingers away from her body. He spun her, holding her captive, and looked down into her face.

'Can you honestly deny I affect you the same way?' he demanded evenly.

On the point of a denial, she felt her heart begin to thump violently and she could only shake her head helplessly.

Randal's hands clasped her face, cupping it between his palms. He gazed deep into her eyes. 'We need each other,' he said softly. 'Forget about love, my sweet. You can make love without ever being in love, you know. There's no reason to be ashamed of the demands of your body. Making love can be a world-shattering experience. Just let it happen. Forget the whole world—only think about this...'

His mouth moved down to possess hers and she groaned, shaking with an overpowering desire for him, her arms locked round his neck, her body pressed hard against his. The grey sky spun overhead. The light vanished. Against her closed eyes an exploding sun seemed to colour the world crimson.

Randal was breathing thickly as he stopped kissing her. His glittering eyes rested briefly on her flushed, sensuous face.

'We have to go back,' he said regretfully. 'We'll set the date for our wedding at this family party. I don't want to wait long—my nerves won't stand it.'

Next day he took her out to buy her a new dress for the party. Laura was shy at the prospect, but he proved an expert at choosing women's clothes. She even teased him about it, saying no doubt he had clothed other women in the past.

'A few,' he admitted shamelessly. His dark face glimmered at her. 'Jealous?'

She went pink and tossed her head. 'Of course not. Why should I care?'

'Why indeed?' he drawled.

He chose a fragile floating silver dress, the straight skirt falling from two thin shoulder-straps without any pretence of a waist. On her slender body it shimmered and glittered like tinsel.

When they got back to her house he made her put it on to show her mother, and later, alone with her downstairs, he took a flat black box out of his pocket and said commandingly, 'Turn round!'

Surprised, she obeyed. He came up behind her and lowered something cold around her slim throat.

She looked down and saw green and silver glinting at her. It was a necklace of emeralds set in silver.

She gasped. 'Good heavens!'

Randal kissed her on the back of her neck. 'I thought it would look good with this dress,' he said in satisfaction.

She turned round to look at him. 'It . . . it looks very valuable. I'll be afraid I shall lose it.'

He slid one of her shoulder-straps down and bent to kiss her creamy shoulder. 'I must go,' he said reluctantly. 'I've got a lot of work to do.'

She saw little of him over the next few days. When he came to collect her and her parents for the party he was devastatingly handsome in an evening suit, his dark face brooding as he looked at her, handing her into the passenger seat next to him.

His London house was alive with lights when they arrived, and Laura remembered with a flicker of excitement her last visit here. The butler, opening the door, showed more humanity than he had on the previous occasion. His eyes surveyed her curiously as Randal, a possessive hand beneath her elbow, moved her past him.

When he moved to take her coat, Randal forestalled him, lifting it away from her and throwing it to him before he slid an arm around her slender waist, his hand closing in an unmistakable gesture of ownership on her.

Flushed and apprehensive, she let him lead her into the room they had seen last time.

It was crowded again, but this time all eyes turned on her like spotlights. Old Mr Mercier hurried forward, hands outstretched. Randal released her and she put her trembling, chilly hands into the old man's.

He was a thin, grey, weary-eyed old man, older than Laura had expected. There was a fragility about him, as if his bones might crack if they were roughly treated. He must be in his seventies, she realised, with a distinct shock. His skin was withered, his eyes sunken. But the tired eyes were alight with pleasure now as he smiled at his son.

'She's beautiful,' he said simply.

As he released her hands, Randal moved closer, once more taking possession of her body, his whole attitude one of triumphant ownership. His father seemed to sum them up with one long look, and a sigh quivered from his lips.

'We are all delighted with this marriage, my dear,' he said. 'Now, you must meet the rest of the family ...'

She moved around the room, clasped to Randal's side like a child, shaking hands, smiling, accepting congratulations. The faces swam before her. She could not remember half the names. But she went through with it somehow, her head held high, her face pale and tense.

Randal had two sisters, both married. They were there with their husbands, all eager to meet the girl Randal had finally chosen. They had waited a long time for this marriage; it had begun to look as though he would never marry. His social life was so busy that a marriage would only have curbed his fun. Now they were mad with curiosity to see the girl who had managed to persuade him that marriage was worth the loss of his freedom.

The eldest, Nicole, was rather like her brother; a dark-haired, strong-faced woman in her forties with cool grey eyes and a piercing smile. Her husband was a stout, balding man of about fifty with a deprecatory smile. There was no doubt who ran that marriage. Nicole only had to look at him to have him leap to her side.

With them was their son, Roddy, and Laura felt herself flush as she recognised the curly-haired medical student whom she had met on that first windy night in the East End.

He didn't seem to recognise her. Had he forgotten, she wondered, or had he been too drunk to remember anything next morning?

He shook hands admiringly and gave Randal a grin. 'Lucky old Randal! She's ravishing.'

Randal's hand tightened on her waist. 'Thank you,' he drawled coolly, but Laura was beginning to know him too well not to hear the cold note in his voice.

His other sister was a comfortable, brown-haired woman with hazel eyes and a cheerful smile. She had two pretty daughters with her. 'Nell and Barbara,' said Randal, with an indifferent wave.

Nell was sixteen, slim, with her mother's colouring and a warm, friendly smile. Barbara was a little older.

She was dark, her face thin and a little aloof, her blue eyes cool as she shook hands.

Their father winked at Laura as she shook hands. 'Randal has all the luck. Where did he find you?'

'Her father is one of our executives,' Randal drawled.

'Trust you to keep it in the firm,' said John Graham. His wife, Arlette, laughed and slapped his arm gently.

'Don't take any notice,' she told Laura with a smile. 'They all try to get at my brother, but Randal is fireproof.'

Later, briefly alone with him, Laura asked him softly, 'Are you fireproof, Randal?'

The grey eyes blazed at her. 'Not where you're concerned,' he said thickly.

She felt a deep pang of satisfaction at having wrung that admission out of him.

'Don't monopolise your beautiful fiancée,' said Roddy, appearing beside them. 'You'll have plenty of time to do that after you're married. When *are* you getting married, by the way?'

Everyone turned to listen, curious to hear the date.

Randal glanced down at Laura. 'I've discussed it with Laura's mother and we think all the arrangements could be made by the beginning of March.'

'So soon?' Nicole looked surprised. Her eyes flickered over Laura's slender silvery figure, lingering on the brilliance of the emeralds which were clasped around her white throat. 'You're in a hurry, aren't you?'

At the hidden implication of the words and that penetrating look, Laura blushed. Did they think she was already pregnant? Perhaps even that she had trapped Randal into marriage?

He looked at his sister icily. 'I'd get married tomorrow

if Laura agreed,' he said flatly. 'As it is, we shall have to wait until the usual rites can be observed.' He glanced at Laura. 'You want the full wedding paraphernalia, don't you?'

She said shyly, 'I suppose it would be nice.'

Or was it somehow a bitter caricature of a marriage she was entering into with him? Should they get married hastily in a register office and skip a church ceremony? She dared not suggest such a thing, anyway; her mother would be too hurt and puzzled. She had to go through with it.

Randal took her up to see his mother, who kissed her warmly and patted her cheek. 'I can't tell you how glad I am,' she said, then her eyes looked gently into Laura's wide green ones. 'Are you sure you are ready for marriage, my dear? You look like a child in that little dress— a beautiful child, but so very young. Randal is so much older than you.'

'You make me sound like a nasty old man, Mother,' he said drily. 'I'm only thirty-six.'

'And she's twenty ...' his mother said.

Randal was watching Laura with that dark brooding look. 'I am going to marry her,' he said stubbornly. 'Don't try to interfere, Mama.'

She sighed. 'Very well. I just wanted to make certain the child knew what she was doing.'

Outside on the landing Randal halted and looked around him irritably. 'I'm sick of this,' he said abruptly. 'There are too damned many members of my family in the house tonight. Come in here.'

He opened a door and Laura followed him into a room, halting as she saw it was a bedroom. She turned, but he had closed the door and was leaning against it, his eyes fixed on her brilliantly.

'Do you mind the difference in our ages?' he asked tersely.

She shook her head, trembling under his stare.

The atmosphere between them grew tense. Randal leaned there, watching her, his eyes compelling.

'Come here,' he said.

Slowly she moved towards him. When she was in his reach, his hands pulled her against him, moulding her slender body against his own.

'Two months is a long time to wait,' he said urgently. 'I seem to have waited years already.'

Feverishly aware of the bed behind them, she trembled, and his hands were still. Against her neck he whispered, 'I want you like hell. Let me love you ...'

'No, please, Randal,' she moaned, hating herself because despite her denial she had felt a sick longing at his words. If he insisted, she was terrified she might give in, her own desire beating up to meet his. She hated him, but she no longer tried to pretend to herself that she did not want him. With a look, a word, a touch, he could arouse a hot sensuality in her.

He pushed her away, his face hard. 'You insist on that damned wedding ring, do you? All right, my sweet, you win—for now. But I'll make you pay for this torture one day, and I'll enjoy every minute of it!'

After the engagement party Laura saw little of him again. He was busy at the firm. Her father had been transferred to another department where he had no contact with finance whatever. James Hallam was not the man to feel miserable for long. He let his wife think he had been promoted, when in fact he had been shunted sideways into a mere sinecure, where he earned a good salary without having any responsibility at all. While Randal was busy at work, Laura was busy with preparations for the wedding.

They engaged an outside firm of caterers, since there would be so many guests, and the reception was to be held in a large hall. Laura singlehandedly made most of the arrangements. She bought her wedding dress and other necessary items, helped her mother to buy a dress for herself and arranged for cars to ferry the guests from the church to the reception.

Randal offered to help with the arrangements, but she firmly refused. Her father was paying for this wedding, and she would see to everything herself, she said. In fact she often regretted it later when she realised how many things she had to do. She had not realised how much was involved in arranging a wedding.

A week beforehand, they had a rehearsal at the church. Laura had chosen two bridesmaids—Nell, Randal's niece, and one of her own cousins, a pretty girl of similar age called Christine.

Laura wore a white woollen dress for the rehearsal. She carefully mimed all the actions, while the vicar explained what would happen, and wondered how she would ever get through the service. The day was approaching faster and faster with the inevitability of death.

Afterwards Randal took her out to dinner. He was terse and offhand all evening, making her dislike him intensely. When they returned to her house she was relieved to be back home.

He turned to her as she prepared to get out of the car. 'Laura,' he said abruptly, then stopped, biting his lip.

'Yes?' she asked questioningly, staring at him.

He paused, then said hurriedly, 'Nothing...' His hands

reached for her. She evaded him, angry that he should expect her to switch on and off like a light bulb. Was this how it was going to be after their marriage?

His face darkened. He ruthlessly jerked her sideways into his arms and kissed her so brutally that she felt the salt taste of blood on her tongue.

His hands moved to her bodice, unbuttoning her dress. She pushed them away violently, but he was too strong for her.

'Don't fight me,' he said savagely. 'I've bought the right to do what I like with you.'

She lay quiescent after that while his mouth crawled over her body, his teeth grazing her naked skin, his hands impatiently demanding.

After a while he lifted his head and looked down at her blankly. She had given him no response whatever, her senses deadened by a feeling of rage.

She asked coldly, 'May I button my dress again now, or haven't you finished?'

His hand slapped her hard across her face. She gave a startled, incredulous cry of pain, and tears sprang to her eyes.

'Don't ever talk to me again in that voice,' he said savagely. 'Do your dress up and get out of here.'

Laura obeyed, her fingers trembling, and ran to the front door, tears falling down her white face.

Her father met her in the hall and looked at her in startled dismay. Then he grinned. 'Lovers' quarrel so soon. Never mind—it's wedding nerves. We all get them. I remember the night before I married your mother . . .'

Laura ran past him and up the stairs to her own room. Flinging herself on the bed, she pounded the pillows with her fists. 'I hate him, I loathe him!' she sobbed soundlessly.

The next week passed too fast. Laura was somehow hoping that something would happen to stop the wedding, some miracle to rescue her. Tom was pale and aloof whenever she saw him, but she dared not ask him for help. She could not involve him in her problems.

Randal never came to the house at all. She was grateful for that small mercy, at least, but it left her in the dark as to his mood, and that worried her a little. Although he had often made love to her before, there had been a brutality in him that night which had frightened her.

The day of their wedding dawned bright and cold. As she walked up the aisle on her father's arm she could see Randal's dark head above the heads of everyone else. She shivered in the damp chill of the stone walls, watching the sunlight fall dustily from high stained glass windows, lying in misty patterns of bright colour on the floor.

The words of the service sounded far away to her, as though they came to her under water. Somehow she made the correct responses. Only Randal knew that as she held out her hand for him to slide his ring on to her finger, she shuddered. His narrowed eyes shot to her face.

They moved back along the church later, past smiling faces. Laura saw Tom in the congregation. His eyes were anxiously concerned. Her feet stumbled as she saw him, and Randal's hand tightened on her arm. She looked up and met his watchful, comprehending gaze.

Enemy, husband, friend, she thought in grim mockery. Perhaps of all those in the church he understood her best.

Always able to read her mind; to know, before she did, what she was feeling.

The organ music swelled triumphantly. The fragrance of her bouquet filled her nostrils. She clung to Randal's arm for fear she fell, her head swimming, her face white and vulnerable.

There seemed to be endless photographs. She smiled and smiled until her facial muscles ached. The photographer called cheerfully, 'How about a kiss, Mr Mercier? Kiss your bride.'

Randal's hand tightened on her waist, he turned her towards him and like an obedient doll she raised her mouth. His lips were gentle, and she was overwhelmed with relief. She could not have borne it if he had kissed her in that cold, brutal fashion again.

They drove to the reception in a car fluttering with white satin ribbons. Randal looked at her dress with a faint smile.

'You're exquisite,' he said softly.

The lustrous white satin was cut low, laying bare her shoulders. Her train was long and floated diaphanously. Her silvery hair was dressed with a coronet of pearls and honeysuckle. Around her neck she wore a silver locket her mother had given her long ago. Inside it was a picture of Tom.

Randal, as if his instincts prompted him, raised a hand to open the locket.

Laura pushed his hand away, her eyes nervous. 'You still haven't told me where we're going on our honeymoon,' she said, trying to distract him.

His eyes narrowed in that disconcerting fashion. He pulled the locket away from her neck and opened it deftly. She watched his face in apprehension.

Suddenly he jerked the chain brutally, hurting her. She felt it snap. Opening the window, he threw the locket out. It glittered in a silver arc as it fell, and she gave a low cry of anger and hurt.

'My mother gave that to me!'

'I warned you I would tolerate no ghosts in my bed,' he said icily.

They arrived at the reception in a bitter silence. Laura had to force a smile as she stood at the door receiving their guests, but she could not make herself smile at Randal, or even look at him.

When everyone had arrived they ate their wedding breakfast, seated at long tables dressed with fine glass and bowls of white and pink carnations, but Laura barely noticed what she ate. One long table was laid out with wedding presents. The silver and glassware glittered in the spring sunlight.

Later the tables were pushed aside for dancing. They cut the cake together, as tradition demanded, and then Randal took her in his arms and spun her on to the floor.

She danced with her head held high, a smile pinned to her lips. No one looking at her would have guessed what emotions ran beneath her fixed mask.

His eyes looked down unsmilingly at her. A muscle twitched in his cheek.

Suddenly she thought of the night ahead, and her body seemed to flame with heat. She shivered and his arm tightened.

'Look at me,' he commanded. 'What is it?'

She flickered a brief glance up at his dark, handsome face, her pulses beating. His eyes narrowed.

'You look remote and untouchable in that dress,' he

murmured in her ear. 'A pity you have to change for the journey. I would enjoy taking it off.'

She was relieved when the music stopped and she could draw away from him. Close contact with his hard, masculine body was too disturbing.

They went to admire their wedding presents. There were so many they had barely looked at most of them. Involuntarily her eye moved to Tom's present—a delicate piece of fine crystal shaped as a white rose in a miniature silver pot. Tom had sent it round to the house yesterday. She had not had a chance to thank him yet.

Seeing where her eyes rested, Randal bent to read the card which leaned against the silver pot.

His grey glance grew chilly. He picked up the beautiful object and balanced it on his palm. 'Quite exquisite,' he said, and his fingers splayed to let it fall to the ground.

Laura's hands clenched into fists at her waist. Her body seemed to be a coiled spring of hatred.

Without looking at her Randal said loudly, 'Oh, how dreadful! I've dropped it. And it was so beautiful ...'

The guests made sympathetic noises, but Randal kicked the pieces under the table and shrugged. 'Never mind, darling,' he said softly, 'I'll get you another one exactly the same.'

She turned, white as her dress. Her eyes sought Tom's, pleading, apologising. Tom was almost as pale as she was, but his gaze gently comforted her across the room.

The dancing began again. The music seemed to crash and thud like thunder. Her head was aching. She wanted to cry, but she couldn't, and so she smiled and smiled until she could have screamed.

'Time to change,' her mother whispered in her ear. She was looking far too flushed and excited, thought Laura anxiously. Following her mother through the crowded hall, she exchanged bright words and smiles with everyone. Then she was alone in a little changing room with her mother. Mrs Hallam kissed her lovingly. 'You looked lovely, darling,' she said.

Laura could have wept.

She changed slowly, not wanting to hurry towards the future. She had chosen to wear a blue suit to go away in; the tight waist-hugging jacket and pleated skirt had a bright, springlike look. Above it her silvery hair was smooth as silk and her green eyes were fever-bright.

She had a last hug with her mother and then went out. Randal was waiting for her, having also changed into a lounge suit. The guests crowded to throw confetti and call good wishes. Randal took her hand and ran with her through them to the car.

His mother was there, in a wheelchair, waiting for a last word. Laura kissed her and was whirled into the car. As it drove away she looked back and saw Tom's white face among the laughing guests. His eyes were blank.

'We're going to Venice,' Randal told her calmly. 'It's my favourite city and I thought you would like it, too.'

'I'm sure I shall,' she said in a polite little voice. She would never forgive him for breaking her crystal rose. It had been an unforgivable thing to do.

They flew to Venice, circling low over the lagoon, their view clouded by mists. Randal had made arrangements for a car to be waiting at the airport. They drove straight to their hotel in time for a rather late dinner.

Laura was tense and sick with nerves. The food tasted like sawdust and ashes in her mouth. Randal insisted that she drink champagne with her meal and the heady wine made her feel dizzy.

After they had eaten they went up to their luxurious suite and Randal indicated their cases lying on the rack beside the door.

'You look tired. I should get to bed if I were you. I'm going out for a stroll. That champagne has given me a headache.'

His tone was reassuringly matter-of-fact. When he had gone she rapidly undressed, took a shower and put on one of her new nightgowns. A white cloud of soft chiffon, it was buttoned to the throat and fell to the floor, completely covering her. She fell into bed and put out the light. She prayed for sleep. If she was asleep when he came back he might go away again. She closed her eyes and let her body relax.

The coolness of the sheets, the warm darkness, helped her to slide down into a gentle doze.

Suddenly the click of the door brought her wide awake. She heard Randal move softly about the room and tried to breath regularly, feigning sleep.

He went into the bathroom and closed the door. Laura lay, listening to the movements she could hear. The door opened again, and yellow light streamed across her face. Quickly she closed her eyes again.

He came towards the bed when he had closed the door. She lay very still, breathing quietly, her mouth as dry as a kiln.

He stood there for a moment, as if listening to her. Then the bedside lamp was suddenly switched on. Her eyes flew open. At once he switched it off again, but not before she had had a flashing image of his face—dark, glimmering, demanding, filled with a ruthless intensity that had stopped her heart.

He slid between the sheets next to her and lay on his side, not moving.

Was he going to go to sleep after all? she wondered. Then his hand moved. She felt it touch her slowly, lapping like fire along her shoulders, arms, the smooth curve of her breast beneath the chiffon.

'What on earth are you wearing?' he asked in grim amusement. 'Is it meant to quench my passion?'

She didn't answer, trying desperately to fight down the desire his wandering fingers had aroused in her.

He moved his hand back to her throat and began to unbutton the nightdress slowly. When he had finished he slid his hand inside her nightdress and moved it caressingly against her. She felt her body arch in sudden hunger. Involuntarily she sighed, the sound loud in the silent room.

'Sit up,' he said abruptly.

She lay there without moving.

He jerked her up by the shoulders. Before she knew what he meant to do he had pulled the nightdress over her head. She gave a cry of surprise and affront and dived under the bedclothes again. She heard him laughing softly.

'Come out, you little rabbit,' he said, his voice deep. He yanked the sheets away and she lay exposed to view, trembling, confused, her heart thudding.

'Are we alone?' he asked, his voice slurred by the champagne or the pressure of his desire.

Laura stared up at the glimmering oval of his face, wondering if he was more drunk than she had supposed.

'I want no memories of Doctor Tom Nicol haunting you tonight,' he said tauntingly.

She was instantly furious. 'Don't even mention his

name,' she said angrily. 'He's worth ten of you ...'

'Maybe, my dear,' he drawled. 'But I am the man in bed with you, and that's the way it's going to stay all night and for every night afterwards.'

She raised her hand to hit him, but his hands came down on her naked shoulders, pushing her back into the pillows. His mouth sought and found hers, and she shook violently under the impact of sudden, searing passion. For a few moments she fought herself and him, wriggling to escape, but his body was too strong and her own desire too powerful. As she relaxed with a smothered sob of self-hatred, his kiss grew gentler, coaxing her, seducing her. Her hands touched his hard chest and slid to his shoulders. She felt their bodies move closer, their limbs tangling. Her hands crept to his back and as he suddenly took her she felt her nails dig into him with pain and spiralling excitement.

She knew now without any shadow of doubt what had stretched between herself and Randal from the beginning. He taught her, in the mounting excitement she felt as his body wrung from hers a fevered abandonment which shattered all her previous conceptions of passion.

'Sweet,' he whispered hoarsely in her ear. 'You're so sweet ... kiss me ...'

She raised her face, kissing him hungrily, her hands still clinging to his naked back, feeling the smoothness of his cool skin under her fingertips with a sensation of sheer sensuality.

Later, as they made love again, the thought arose suddenly in her mind: would it have been like this with Tom? Could he ever have made her whole body melt in this languid sweetness?

She pushed the thought away, shuddering, as though at

a blasphemy, and for a moment her body was unresponsive under Randal's experimental hands.

'What is it?' he asked her huskily. 'Darling, did I hurt you?' Then he tensed. His fingers crawled over her eyes, cheeks, lips, exploring with tactile delicacy, as though, like a blind man, he could read the secrets of her mind at his fingertips.

He swore savagely. 'I warned you once. Do I have to crush the thought of him out of your thick little skull?' Then he began to kiss her in that brutal, barbarous fashion, his teeth biting her lips, his mouth leaving bruises on her soft inner skin.

She fought him, striking his back with clenched fists. Arching over her, his body pale in the darkness, he stared down at her.

'Don't push me too far, Laura. Sometimes I feel I could kill you,' he said thickly.

'You said you didn't mind who had my heart so long as you could have my body,' she reminded him bitterly.

'I said too damned much,' he said savagely. 'How can I make love to a woman who is thinking of another man?'

'The answer's simple,' she flung. 'Stop making love to me.'

'You wouldn't like that,' he said mockingly. He bent his head and kissed her. 'You enjoy it too much.'

Her rage dissolved in treacherous weakness. Her body leapt into clamouring life wherever his lips touched. Her hands twisted into his back, her fingertips caressed slowly along the line of his spine, following the faint marking hair which etched out the curve. She arched herself against him, groaning.

'You want me, don't you?' Randal whispered, his tongue moving against the shell of her ear.

'Yes, yes,' she moaned in a rising tide of madness, surrendering.

'It's time you learnt to know yourself,' Randal said thickly. 'Your body was created for this, and tonight I'm going to teach you everything your body craves for...'

CHAPTER SEVEN

SHE woke up to a room full of sunlight and a feeling of incredible lightness, as though her body was floating on air. Instantly she remembered the previous night. Randal's naked body was curved close against her, one arm flung possessively across her back, her cheek pillowed on his bare chest. She lay very still, listening to the regular beat of his heart beneath her ear. Then very carefully she slid herself way and sat up, pulling the sheet around her breasts, looking at him curiously.

What was he really like, this disturbing dark stranger who had explored her body and her senses so persistently last night, showing her a side of her own nature she still found terrifying and shocking?

His face was relaxed in sleep, the long mouth vulnerable, the hard brown jawline faintly darkened with overnight stubble. Her eyes moved down to the sprawled body, and her heart quickened involuntarily, remembering things she wished she could forget.

Suddenly without a word, without raising his lids, Randal put out a compelling hand and pulled her back against him.

'Pleasant dreams?' he drawled, his mouth touching her temple. 'You slept like a baby.'

'How do you know?' she asked, already finding her traitorous body adjusting pleasurably to the curve of his.

'I woke up hours ago,' he said with a smothered

chuckle. 'You were dead to the world, which gave me a chance to admire my wife without interruption.'

She wondered how long he had been awake. Did he know that she had been looking at him just now?

'What are we going to do today?' she asked nervously.

His soft laughter made her blush. 'Stay here,' he said teasingly. 'And carry on from where we left off ...'

She ignored that. 'I want to explore Venice,' she said.

'I want to explore you,' he replied promptly. 'Venice can wait. It has been there for hundreds of years. It can afford to wait. You've only been in my bed for one night and I'm far from tired of making love to you.'

'I'm hungry,' she complained. 'I want my breakfast.'

'What a mundane little mind you have,' he said softly. His hand moved over the naked swell of her hips. 'Your skin's like satin. Did you know you have a tiny mole right in the centre of your back?'

'Of course I knew,' she said.

'I didn't,' he told her, his fingers feeling for it. 'It was one of the enchanting surprises you had in store for me.' His mouth suddenly descended on her surprised lips, coaxing them apart. He pushed her down into the bed, his body hard and demanding, and Laura gave up all pretence of wanting to eat breakfast. Her lids closed, her body pressed languorously against him and she submitted.

Later they showered and dressed to go down for lunch. By now she was ravenous and she looked hungrily at the delicious meal which was served to them in the cool, marble-floored dining-room.

Randal grinned as she finished her meal. 'Love gives you an appetite, I see.'

She was instantly scarlet, terrified the waiter would

have overheard. 'Ssh!' she whispered angrily. 'Someone will hear you.'

He leaned back lazily in his chair, his whole body relaxed and satisfied. 'Oh, Italians understand love. They take it as easily as they take the rest of life. It's we Anglo-Saxons who make such heavy weather of it.'

She sipped her coffee, the surface foaming with whipped cream. 'Can we go out and look at Venice now?' she asked.

'Why not?' he shrugged. 'We'll start with a ride in a gondola. You'll like that. The perfect honeymoon experience.'

Floating along on the Grand Canal later, she gazed up with delight at the great Venetian palaces they passed, a glory of cream and pink and pale blue. Decaying though they were, they still held an incredible beauty, dreamlike as clouds reflected in the water, their gilding weather-worn, their masonry crumbling. As they passed one Randal leaned over to study it with a little more interest.

'A friend of mine lives there,' he explained.

'What's his name?' she asked. 'Is he a Venetian nobleman?'

Randal flickered a curious glance at her. 'She's an American widow,' he drawled. 'Her husband made paper clips and when he died she sold the company and came to Venice to live in style.'

Jealousy twisted inside her, making her skin suddenly pale. 'What's her name?' she asked, trying to make her tone light.

'Antoinette,' he said, making it sound deliciously French. 'Antoinette Bell.'

'Is she pretty?' Laura trailed her fingers in the water, pretending an indifference she did not feel.

'Ravishing,' Randal said in a voice which seemed to hold the echo of a remembered pleasure.

'You must look her up while we're here,' she said, turning the point of a knife of pain into her flesh.

'Excellent idea,' he drawled. 'I'll ring her when we get back to the hotel.'

They landed at the Piazza San Marco and walked around the uneven square watching the pigeons fly up into the blue sky, their wings clattering. He showed her round St Mark's and then they had a cool glass of lemon at a table in a café. There were arcades of shops behind the square. They wandered through them, window shopping. Randal insisted on buying her a white silk head square and tried to buy her a piece of exquisite Venetian glass, but she refused, angrily remembering his destruction of Tom's wedding present.

When they got back to the hotel Randal lifted the telephone in their suite and rang Antoinette Bell. Laura went into the bathroom to wash and change her dress.

When she emerged, slight as a willow in a green linen dress, Randal stood by the window in his shirt sleeves, staring out at the twilight city.

He turned and looked at her, his face a tormenting mask. 'Are you hungry again?' he asked lightly. 'We could have an early dinner if you like. We've been invited to a party at Antoinette's house tonight. I thought you might like the experience of visiting an old Venetian palace, so I accepted.'

Coldly she shrugged. 'If you like.'

'It was your idea I ring her,' he pointed out.

You didn't have to jump at the idea, she thought jealously. Aloud, she said, 'Shall we go down, then?'

He shouldered into his jacket and nodded. The dining-room was half empty at that hour and the waiter looked surprised to see them. A shadow of amusement in his glance made Laura realise that he knew they were honeymooners. She blushed and stared at her plate, her hand nervously fiddling with a bread stick.

She ate far less at this meal, playing with her veal, her stomach protesting at the idea of eating.

Randal watched her across the table, talking lightly of Venice and the slow daily destruction of the city. 'Incredible to imagine a world without Venice,' he said. 'They really ought to do something before it's too late, but the task is so immense.'

They emerged from their hotel half an hour later to find the city plunged into shimmering blue warmth. The sun had set and night fallen, but somehow the lights of the gondolas and the sky reflections in the illuminated water, made the night seem as bright as day. They floated slowly along the canal. A faintly unpleasant odour crept out to them from the side canals. Their gondolier skimmed expertly to the private landing stage outside Antoinette Bell's palace. Randal leapt up the steps and then turned to help Laura alight. She stumbled on the top step and fell against him, her hair brushing his chin.

She felt his body suddenly tense. Her own senses were leaping. Even so a brief contact made her heart thud in excitement.

They walked up the last steps to the door. From within came dreamy Italian popular music, sweet as melted honey. Antoinette Bell came to greet them as her servant showed them into the high-ceilinged room in which the party was being held.

She was a woman of about thirty-five, her hair a rich chestnut in which gold tints glittered, her eyes heavily outlined in green eye-shadow, their brown-purple depths slumbrously smiling as she kissed Randal, her hands linked behind his head.

'Honey, it's so good to see you,' she said in an American drawl. 'Long time no see. What have you been doing with yourself, getting married and all? I thought you were a confirmed bachelor.'

'We all come to it in the end,' Randal said lightly. 'Antoinette, this is my wife, Laura.'

Antoinette turned her eyes on Laura and raised a plucked eyebrow. 'My God,' she drawled, 'she's a dreamy little dolly. I never figured you for a cradle-snatcher, Randal darling.'

Randal's face tightened, but he smiled, his eyes glittering. 'Catch them young and treat them rough,' he murmured cynically.

Antoinette laughed softly. 'Poor Laura!' She wound her hand through Randal's arm. 'Come and meet some of my friends.' Laura angrily followed them across the wide room, feeling distinctly unnecessary.

Antoinette stopped at a little group of young people. Waving her hand negligently at Laura, she said to one young man, 'This is Laura. She wants to dance.'

Randal looked at Laura briefly. She felt his glance but did not look at him. With a sweet smile she let the young man lead her away.

As they circled the floor among the other dancers she studied her partner curiously. He was a handsome boy of her own age, his smooth olive skin glowing golden in the artificial light, his black eyes admiring her openly.

'Antoinette didn't tell me your name,' she said.

'Gian-Carlo,' he said, his voice musical.

'What do you do, Gian-Carlo?'

He frowned. 'What do I do?'

'For a job,' she explained.

He smiled, white teeth flashing. 'I am *studente*,' he said. 'A student. I study ...' he paused, searching for the word, 'history of buildings.'

'Architecture?'

'Yes,' he nodded. 'In Venice there are many such to study. I am born here. All around me ... old buildings dying ... I like to know about them.'

Laura nodded. 'I can understand that. Venice is very beautiful.'

'Not so beautiful as you,' he said, his voice softening to an amorous drawl.

She laughed, lifting her green eyes to his face. 'Careful, Gian-Carlo! I'm on my honeymoon.'

He looked incredulously at her. 'You are?' His dark eyes were filled with regret. 'But where is your husband?'

She glanced over towards Randal who was talking to Antoinette by a high window. As she looked at him his grey eyes suddenly flicked over towards her. She looked away quickly.

'That is your husband?' Gian-Carlo asked in surprise. 'But I know him ...' Then he bit the words off, flushing.

She glanced at him curiously. 'You do?' She wondered what had made him colour. 'He's an old friend of Antoinette's,' she said.

'Yes,' Gian-Carlo said blankly.

She suspected he was hiding something. What did he know that she did not?

As they moved away she saw Randal and Antoinette reflected in one of the long gilt-framed mirrors which hung on the walls. Antoinette was talking to Randal, a slight smile on her full red mouth, her hand resting lightly on his sleeve. Randal bent, lifting her hand, and kissed it softly. Antoinette's hand moved upward to his lean dark face, curving against the outline of his jaw. She leaned forward and kissed him very briefly. Then Gian-Carlo whirled Laura away and she saw nothing else.

It was enough, she thought bitterly. Enough to tell her what she had already suspected. Antoinette had once been very close to Randal. Was she his mistress? There had been old intimacy in their kiss.

It was one thing to know that he had had other women. It was quite another to see him with one.

Gian-Carlo brought her back to the side of the room where Randal and Antoinette stood. Another young man stepped forward, grinning at him. 'Excuse, please,' he said, cutting in, and floated Laura away in his arms.

She danced several dances in a row with Gian-Carlo's friends. They were remarkably similar in their approaches. She quickly learnt to parry their flirtatious remarks, teasing them lightly and coolly.

One of them led her to a long line of chairs, seated her and vanished, returning quickly with some cherry-flavoured icecream in a glass dish and a tall drink of lemon flavoured with something that sent a wave of heat through her body.

She sat chatting to her escort for a quarter of an hour, letting the ice slip deliciously down her throat, sipping her drink.

Then Randal appeared in front of her. He grinned casually at the boy beside her. 'Will you excuse me if I dance with my wife?' he asked idly.

The boy looked aghast and leapt up, stammering something. Randal laughed and looked down at her, his grey eyes masked.

Laura put down her drink and stood up. His hand closed on her waist, pulling her against him.

They circled without speaking for a while. She could feel the hard masculinity of his body move against her and her heart was suddenly pounding with excitement. In the mirrors she saw their reflections move hazily, her head close to his shoulder, his arm holding her tightly.

She ventured a secret glance up at his face, her lashes lowered to hide the expression in her eyes. A slow languor was invading her body as they danced. She thought of the long night ahead and her legs trembled.

He looked down at her, his face dark and remote. The grey eyes skimmed her face.

'How well do you know Antoinette?' she asked in a voice she tried to drain of all feeling.

His mouth twitched. 'Why?'

She shrugged. 'I just wondered...'

'Curious? Or jealous? Or both?' he asked mockingly.

The music ended before she had any need to reply, and she was thankful for that. Because as he asked the question she knew quite certainly that she was not only jealous, she was bitterly jealous.

They moved back towards Antoinette. She looked at Randal, her huge brown eyes warmly inviting.

'Would you mind if we leave now?' he asked, to Laura's surprise. 'I've got a shocking headache. Too much vintage champagne, I fear.'

Antoinette's face filled with sympathy. 'Oh, poor darling...' She kissed him on the mouth, her hand patting his cheek. 'Take two aspirins, now, and lay off the champagne.'

They returned to their hotel in almost total silence. Laura wondered angrily what Randal was thinking about so intently, staring up at the dark night sky with its purple bloom and scatter of steely stars.

As he closed the door of their suite Laura asked, 'Shall I find you that aspirin?'

'What aspirin?' he asked, staring at her blankly.

'You said you had a headache,' she reminded him.

'I was lying,' he shrugged.

She was puzzled. 'Why?'

'I wanted to leave,' he explained as if she were a child.

'I thought you were enjoying the party,' she said, bewildered and surprised.

He came behind her and unzipped her dress, sliding the narrow shoulder-straps down over her shoulders. Her heart began to race as his mouth burned down on her bare skin. 'I saw your face,' he said softly. 'I knew what you were thinking. I told you I could read your mind.'

She was suffused with heat, her body trembling as he pulled her back to lean against him, his hands moving expertly over her.

'What was I thinking?' she asked huskily.

He turned her round into his arms and began to kiss her slowly, his lips persuasive. She made a sound deep in her throat and her arms curved round his neck, pulling his head down.

'Undo my shirt,' he murmured against her mouth.

Later, her body aching with his passionate possession of her, she lay cradled on him, her mouth against his naked shoulder. 'Tell me about Antoinette,' she murmured suddenly.

She felt him laugh, his chest heaving. 'Women are like ferrets. They never give up until they've explored every bolthole.'

'Were you her lover?' she insisted.

'Would you mind if I were?'

'I thought we agreed that we would leave each other's hearts free,' she murmured. 'You said you didn't want my love, just my body. Why shouldn't I feel the same?'

He lay very still. 'Do you?' he asked roughly.

She did not answer. She couldn't because she didn't know the answer.

'So you wouldn't mind if I had been Antoinette's lover?' he asked, his tone odd. She could no longer see his face and so she could not probe his features for some clue to his feelings. 'It doesn't matter to you if I've done this to her, too ...' His mouth moved sensuously along her bare shoulder, sending waves of pleasure mounting to her head. 'You really don't give a damn, do you, my sweet amoral little darling?' His voice stabbed at her, and with each word she felt a terrible desolation. She could not tolerate the thought of him in bed with another woman.

At the realisation she felt a wince of bitter pain, and on the heels of that another more terrible than anything she had ever experienced before, a pain which left her numb with self-discovery.

Oh, God, she thought, dazedly, I've fallen in love with him somehow.

For a moment she tried to reject the idea, conjuring up the image of Tom to defeat it, but Tom's face had escaped her and all she could think of was Randal, sweeping her away from the safety of ignorance into the dangerous waters of passion, teaching her the life of the senses and in the process making her fall helplessly in love. What she had believed to be love for Tom had been a gentle first experiment, inextricably mixed with hero-worship and mere fondness. Her heart had known itself under threat from Randal at once, even though her mind was blind to his danger.

She hazarded a glance at him as he leaned above her. The grey eyes were watching her with a strange expression, eager and wary at once. Whatever happened, she thought suddenly, with certainty, he must never guess. If he knew she had fallen in love with him how he would mock and crow at her! She had said so much about her pure, noble love for Tom! She had sworn she could never fall in love with him. Randal would be cynically amused, possibly even embarrassed, if he knew her new feelings.

'What are you thinking?' he asked intently. 'Why are you so quiet?' His dark face smiled at her teasingly. 'Don't tell me you really are jealous of Antoinette?'

'I was remembering something Gian-Carlo said tonight,' she murmured lightly.

'Gian-Carlo?' His face darkened. 'Which of those amorous Italians was he? The one feeding you ice-cream?'

'No, the first one I danced with,' she said. 'A very handsome boy.'

'Was he indeed?' Randal's hands took her shoulders and flung her on to her back. 'I won't have you thinking of other men while you're in my bed,' he said grimly. 'I've told you that before ...'

His mouth came down to claim hers and she gave herself up eagerly, responding with all the new fire her discovery of her love for him had set blazing inside her. Randal gasped against her mouth and tightened his possessive grip, crushing her slight body under him.

Before he drove all other thoughts from her head, Laura wondered desperately how long she could bear to love a man whose only interest in her was the possession of her body. She had accepted that condition unthinkingly. Now she knew it was going to be an intolerable situation.

They stayed in Venice for two weeks. Randal showed Laura all the old churches, the fine palaces and public buildings, took her to the Lido to swim and sunbathe, took her exploring the Lagoon by boat while the sun made the white mist shimmer with heat. The days passed rapidly, but the darkness did not come a moment too soon for her fevered senses. She was becoming obsessed with him, her heart thumping once they closed the door on the world and were alone, her blood racing round her body, her senses leaping passionately to life at his touch.

The urgency of his lovemaking did not seem to lessen as time went by. Almost, she felt, he was waiting for something, watching for some response from her which never came. She felt he was driving himself implacably as if to prove something. But what?

Once she wondered if it might be possible that he loved her, but although she watched his dark face intently he gave no sign of emotion as he made love to her. His passion was white-hot but strangely unemotional. At times she even thought he regarded her as an object rather than a person. He would stroke her body gently, exclaiming over the whiteness of her skin or the smoothness of her round breasts, more as if he were describing a piece of delicate china than a woman.

Spending so much time alone with him she was gradually becoming acquainted with his hidden character. He was surprisingly kind, generous to a fault, enjoying the purchase of small gifts for her. Every day he bought her some present, sometimes jewellery, sometimes a simple thing like a box of chocolates. He was an easy companion, charming and amusing, his conversation unfailingly pleasant.

Passing a street artist near St Mark's, he insisted on having her portrait drawn, and seemed delighted with what the artist produced.

'When we get home we'll have a real portrait painted,' he said seriously. 'You have fine cheekbones. You would make a wonderful picture.'

On their last day in Venice he was reluctant to get up in the morning, sensuously engaged in his ceaseless exploration of her body.

'Shouldn't we get up?' she yawned, stretching like a sun-warmed cat.

His hand halted on her stomach. 'Am I boring you?' he asked with sudden savagery.

She looked at him through her gold-tipped lashes. 'Did I say you were? All I said was . . .'

'I know what you said,' he said starkly. 'Don't look at me in that flirtatious way, or I'll take you again to teach you a lesson you won't forget.'

'It is our last day,' she pointed out, her blood stirring at his threat.

'Then we'll spend it here in bed,' he said hoarsely, kissing her shoulder.

'I want my breakfast,' she denied him, sliding suddenly out of the bed and running into the bathroom. When she had showered she went back into the room. He was lying on his stomach, his face buried in the pillows. He looked as if he was asleep, so she got dressed quickly.

When she turned round she found him watching her expressionlessly. 'Aren't you going to get up?' she asked.

'Go down,' he said crisply. 'I'll follow.'

She got the impression something was bothering him, but she said nothing, shrugging. She went down to breakfast and just as she finished her meal he joined her, slim and dynamic in a thin blue shirt and grey trousers.

After this odd beginning he proved his usual self, enjoying her pleasure in the beautiful city, teasing her, laughing at her, talking lightly as they made a farewell tour of Venice.

That night for the first time he did not make love to her. She lay in the warm darkness, wide awake, wondering what was wrong and worrying anxiously about the future. Their marriage was founded on that one tie between them. If Randal was now tired of her, sated by two weeks of unceasing lovemaking, what would happen to their marriage?

CHAPTER EIGHT

LONDON looked grey and uninviting when they got back. They drove along the motorway in Randal's long-nosed limousine, the silver mascot on the bonnet glittering, sweeping through the other traffic with a soft purring of the engine the only sound. Randal's face was suddenly strange to her again, the eagle profile set in thought as he drove, his eyes on the road and his mind God knew where but certainly not on her. Laura leaned back in her seat, wrapped in a short pure white fur jacket he had had waiting for her in the car—a post-honeymoon present, he had explained, throwing it to her with a casual gesture, as though it was a mere nothing, the sort of trinket you might bestow on a child, instead of being the most expensive garment she had ever worn in her life: white mink, rare and exquisitely styled, lined with shimmering silvery silk, bearing the label of a famous Bond Street furrier. He must have bought it before they left, she realised. The car had been driven to meet them at the airport by the Mercier company chauffeur. Randal had left him to deal with their luggage while he strode through the airport to the car-park, then when the unfortunate man came struggling along to the car with a trolley laden with their cases, he informed him in a cavalier fashion that he was to make his own way back to the London office. They had driven away leaving the man gloomily gazing after them.

'Poor man!' Laura had protested.

Randal's dark brows had lifted. 'He'll put it on expenses,' he shrugged. 'And it will take him away from work for a few hours.'

'Do you always treat your staff so high-handedly?'

The grey eyes contemplated her coolly. 'My staff work for me, not the other way around. I tell them what I want them to do and they do it, or leave my employment. Why should I pay them to do what they want to do?'

'No wonder my father used to call you ...' She broke off, realising herself on the brink of an indiscretion which might ruin his relationship with her father.

The hard mouth twitched derisively. 'That young swine Mercier?' he murmured.

She gasped. 'You knew?'

'Your father is inclined to say what he thinks in a voice which carries all over the building,' Randal drawled. 'I would have had to be deaf not to know.'

After that, they had lapsed into this long silence. She stared out at the green countryside with pleasure. It seemed a long time since she had last seen England. After the glory of Venice in the spring, all pink and gold, decay and beauty mingled so inextricably, England was a calm and tranquil place. Old barns of red brick, dreaming elms which traced infinity with their budding leaves, small villages of neat houses, criss-crossed with narrow country lanes which wound drunkenly from hamlet to hamlet across the landscape.

As they entered the metropolitan complex of grey brick and huddled streets, her spirits fell lower. Compared to what they had left, this was a desert land. On their honeymoon they had had laughter, lazy spring days, the endless pleasures of mutual discovery. Now they were returning to ordinary life, the day-to-day routine.

Until they found a house of their own it had been agreed that they should stay in the large white Mayfair house which had been Randal's home for years. Mrs Mercier had set aside the whole of the second floor for them, giving them an enormous suite of rooms to themselves, which would involve the servants in a great deal of rearrangement. Mrs Mercier herself had changed bedrooms, moving into a large room on the ground floor. When Laura protested at this inconvenience to her mother-in-law, Mrs Mercier had smiled at her and said she was secretly delighted. 'It's really much better for me to have a room on the ground floor, but habit is stronger than common sense. I've had that bedroom for years. It never occurred to me before to change it.'

When their car drew up outside the house, the butler appeared in the porch, a faint smile on his usually wooden face. Randal grinned at him, accepting his murmured congratulations with a calm nod.

He steered Laura into the house where his parents were awaiting them eagerly. Shyly she bent to kiss her mother-in-law's cheek, and Mrs Mercier's grey eyes, so like her son's, studied her closely.

'You look very pretty, my dear,' she told her approvingly.

Mr Mercier folded her in a close embrace, patting her shoulder. 'It's nice to have you home again,' he said, and for the first time she noted a very slight French accent, more an echo of intonation than anything since his English was completely fluent.

'Take Laura up to the suite,' said Randal's mother to him. 'And when you've washed your hands, bring her down for a sherry before dinner.'

Randal pushed open the door of their bedroom and

waved her through. Laura stood there, entranced, staring around the room. She had been shown it by Mrs Mercier before her wedding day. Then it had been totally empty, the floor uncarpeted, the walls echoing. During their honeymoon, she now discovered, there had been a major work of redecoration carried out. Now the room was carpeted in ice-blue, the walls were painted white, with a thin gold stripe outlining oval plaster medallions at regular intervals, and new furniture had been brought in, the white and gold of the Louis Quinze period, with frail curved legs and bow fronts. Walking over to the dressing-table, she sat down on a matching stool upholstered in blue quilted silk and played dreamily with the expensive toiletries laid out before her.

Randal took off his jacket and tossed it on the bed, disappearing into the bathroom which led out of their room. She heard him washing, the water splashing. He stood in the doorway, a towel in his hands, watching her as she picked up a large bottle of French perfume.

'Try it,' he suggested, tossing the towel back into the bathroom and sauntering behind her.

She sprayed a little behind her ears. He bent, his hands on her shoulders, and inhaled the scent. 'Mm ... delicious. Sweet and unsophisticated ...'

'Like me,' she said, a trifle bitterly.

His face lifted, appearing oddly unfamiliar in the mirror. Their eyes met in the reflection. 'You sound as if you regret the fact,' he said. 'Sophistication is just the veneer time applies to people. You haven't yet acquired it, thank God.'

'Unlike Antoinette Bell,' she suggested.

His eyes held hers, that now familiar wary, watchful look in them. 'Why bring her up again?'

She shrugged, her eyes dropping. 'She's sophisticated.'

'She's been around a long time,' he said casually. His left hand dropped out of sight behind her back. She heard her zip slide down. He pushed her dress down over her shoulders and lifted her from the stool, his lips brushing her bare flesh lightly. 'You'd better get changed,' he said coolly. 'My father keeps punctual meals. He gets annoyed if anyone is late for dinner.'

She was oddly shy of him in this new setting, as though the intimacy of their honeymoon had vanished when they left Venice. She felt as if he was a stranger again, and the idea of changing her dress in front of him made her nervous, so she selected a dress from her suitcase and went into the bathroom, saying, 'I must wash first . . .'

Randal's mouth quirked teasingly. 'Don't tell me you're shy!'

She ignored the question, flushing. When she re-emerged he was wearing a different suit and brushing his sleek dark hair while he stood in front of the mirror. He turned to survey her from head to toe.

'Very charming,' he murmured, but with a slightly ironic undertone.

She had chosen to wear a dress which made her look even younger, a demur little dove-grey creation, very expensive since he had insisted she go to a Bond Street shop to buy her dresses, but somehow conveying a nun-like modesty, the bodice styled with a high neckline whose lacy collar hinted at a ruff, pearl buttons leading down to the tight waist, skirts which flared as she walked, and long tight sleeves which ended in pearl-buttoned lace cuffs.

'You look as if you stepped right out of a Quaker girls' school,' he commented drily. 'My parents will wonder if I snatched you straight from your classroom.'

'Don't you like it?' She was uncertain at once, eyeing herself in the mirror. He shrugged without replying.

She tidied her fine, silvery hair with trembling hands, delaying the moment when they must go down to join his family. The honeymoon had been a magic interlude. Now they were back in reality, and she was not sure she could cope with it. Randal himself seemed so different, the hot-blooded, passionate lover submerged in the cool business man.

'Before we go down we ought to look at the rest of the suite,' she said quickly. 'Your mother will want to know what we think of it.'

He nodded. 'That's true. Come on, but hurry ...'

They opened all the doors, peering in at the rooms briefly. Laura was delighted with the little kitchenette which had been installed—a narrow boxroom had been cleverly converted with fitted cabinets and all the necessary cooking equipment; an electric oven, a hob, a tall, slim refrigerator. Apple green and cream, the room welcomed her warmly. She could imagine cooking meals for Randal in here, doing the work she had always done at home and which she knew she was good at. For the first time she could envisage life here with him. She was not accustomed to an idle life. She needed to do something. She had to be necessary to someone.

Yet she could not help feeling slightly anxious. His family had gone to so much trouble and expense. Did they secretly hope that she and Randal would stay here instead of looking for a house of their own? She had been looking forward to finding a place which would belong to them and no one else. She liked his parents very much, but married people should have as much privacy as possible, and what real privacy could they ever have sharing this house with Mr and Mrs Mercier, not to mention the servants who also slept under this capacious roof?

When they entered the sitting-room they found his parents waiting for them, one eye on the clock. Mr Mercier looked hard at Randal. 'You've cut it a bit fine,' he said brusquely.

Randal poured two glasses of sherry and handed one to Laura. She held the delicate crystal stem nervously, sipping the amber liquid, feeling the warmth of it enter her body.

'What did you think of the suite?' Randal's mother asked her, leaning forward in her wheelchair, her hands resting on the padded arms.

'It's marvellous,' she said shyly. 'You've been very kind. Going to so much trouble ... our bedroom is really charming, and the kitchenette has been so cleverly built ...'

Mrs Mercier looked pleased. 'Whenever you feel like cooking a meal up there, I hope you will do so,' she said warmly. 'But we shall be delighted to have you eating with us as often as you like. It's entirely up to you. I expect some evenings when Randal is working late you won't feel like cooking for yourself, you know. I remember feeling like that myself. On those evenings you must come down to us, Laura. The food will always be here, and we shall be very happy to have your company.'

'We're only just back from our honeymoon,' said Randal a trifle sharply. 'Don't start talking as if I'd deserted her already!'

His mother shot him a curious look. 'I know how involved you get at work. How many evenings have you forgotten to come home for dinner? I just want Laura to know she's always welcome with us.'

'Good,' he said disagreeably. 'Laura, drink your sherry. You've hardly tasted it.'

Flushing, she drained the glass and put it down on the silver tray. He seemed on edge tonight, and she wondered why. Could it be because he was beginning to regret their hasty marriage? Had he married her simply to get her into bed, and having achieved his objective was he wishing he had not committed himself so irrevocably to her?

They ate dinner in a long, quietly decorated dining-room, the oval satinwood table shining in the candle-light. Candelabra were placed all the way down the centre. Around them were grouped bowls of fruit and flowers. The meal was served discreetly by the butler, who had a sixth sense about topping up glasses or whipping away the plates.

Laura barely noticed what she ate. Pushing the food around on her plate, she attempted to disguise her lack of appetite, but Randal's acute eye missed nothing.

'Aren't you hungry?' he demanded as if she were a child.

Mrs Mercier looked from one to the other of them, frowning. 'Leave the child alone, Randal. It's her first night back. Of course she's nervous. She's in new surroundings and has to adjust to us. You seem to forget, we're almost strangers to her.' She smiled affectionately at Laura. 'Take no notice of him, my dear. My son can be brutal at times. If you aren't hungry, leave it. It really doesn't matter.'

The butler softly removed her plate as she was hesitating. She looked at Randal's remote profile with anxiety.

The sweet course was served next. The butler hovered

behind her chair, showing her the delectable-looking chilled raspberry pudding, a smooth pink texture with swirls of whipped cream and fresh raspberries as decoration.

'Nursery food,' Randal said distastefully, eating a spoonful. 'Is this especially for Laura?'

His mother looked at him indignantly. 'Eat your meal and be quiet,' she commanded.

Laura tasted the pudding and was appreciative. 'It's delicious,' she told her mother-in-law. The icy cold mixture slid down her hot throat, leaving the sweet sharpness of the fruit on her tongue.

'We'll take coffee in the sitting-room,' Mrs Mercier told the butler, who bowed silently.

Mr Mercier stood up slowly, his back bowed. 'Will you excuse me if I don't have any coffee, my dear?' he asked his wife. 'I'm tired, and I would like to go to bed.'

She looked at him with concern. 'Of course not, Yves. You look pale. I hope you're not going to start another cold. They pull you down so quickly.'

He smiled at her. 'I think it's just the excitement of the day,' he said simply. He looked at Laura. 'I've been very happy to see you under my roof, my dear child. I hope you'll be as happy here as we have been.'

She went to him and kissed his cheek, her slight, curved figure raised on tiptoe to reach his face. 'Thank you for being so kind to me.'

'You make it easy to be kind,' he said, with a smile. 'You're a sweet child.'

Mrs Mercier turned her wheels towards the door. 'I'll see you to bed, Yves,' she said. 'I'll come back for my coffee, Randal. Go into the sitting-room and I'll join you later.'

Randal and Laura went obediently to the sitting-room. The curtains were drawn, the lamps lit, an electric log fire burnt in the fireplace. Randal looked down into her face as they walked towards the hearth.

'You've a crumb of that ridiculous raspberry pudding on your upper lip,' he said.

Blushing, she put out her tongue to lick it away, but he shook his head. 'It's still there,' he said. 'Here, stand still . . .'

She raised her face, expecting him to produce a handkerchief to wipe it away, but instead he bent his head and his tongue softly removed it from her mouth.

Scarlet rushed into her face as the butler quietly entered the room behind them. She turned away and stared blindly at the log fire. She heard the clink of coffee cups, the rattle of spoons.

'I'll do that,' Randal said curtly.

Then she heard the butler's quiet footsteps depart and the door closed with a soft swish.

Randal poured the coffee and brought her a cup. She stirred it without looking at him. 'Sit down,' he said tersely. 'And stop jumping like a rabbit every time I come near you. What's the matter with you? I thought you were cured of that habit in Venice.'

She didn't answer. There was nothing she could say. She sipped her coffee and longed to hear Mrs Mercier arrive.

Randal lounged beside the mantelpiece, his brooding gaze fixed on the bright top of her head. 'What are you planning to do with yourself tomorrow?' he asked suddenly.

She looked up then, green eyes wide. 'I thought I should visit my parents,' she said.

'Where by a strange coincidence you'll meet Dr Tom Nicol too,' he said in sudden savagery.

Laura's face glowed, and she looked down again.

'You'll remember that you're now married, won't you?' he asked her in that unpleasant voice. 'There are certain rules which apply to a married woman. She doesn't carry on just as she did when she was single.'

'The same applies to men,' she pointed out.

Then the butler opened the door and wheeled Mrs Mercier into the room. Randal moved to pour his mother some coffee, kissing her cheek as he handed it to her.

'What's that for?' Mrs Mercier asked him with amusement.

'All the care you've taken with our suite,' he said lightly. 'Thank you. We couldn't be more pleased.'

'I'm glad you like it,' she said, her eyes smiling. 'I realise, of course, that you'll not be there long. You'll be looking for a place of your own.'

'We're in no hurry,' Randal said casually.

Mrs Mercier looked delighted. 'Of course, it will help Laura to slide more easily into her new role,' she said warmly. 'Running a house is a difficult job for a young girl. She can get used to the idea at her leisure here.'

'That had occurred to me,' Randal nodded.

His mother smiled across the room at Laura. 'I do hope you'll feel free to entertain as much as you like,' she said. 'You won't disturb us. It will be nice to have some life in the house. We're too quiet, I often think.'

'I hope you'll let me entertain you and Mr Mercier,' Laura suggested shyly. 'I shall make you my first guests.'

Mrs Mercier laughed delightedly. 'That would be lovely. Can you cook, my dear?'

'Laura is a first-rate cook,' Randal said.

DISTURBING STRANGER 143

Laura flushed. 'I'm not exactly Cordon Bleu,' she objected quietly. 'But I have done quite a bit of cooking.' She was feeling slightly apprehensive as she listened to them discuss her future. It sounded as if Randal did not intend to change his way of life an inch. Did he expect her to go on living here for ever, a permanent house guest in his parents' home, without responsibilities or duties? She knew she would hate it. She was so used to running a house with all its attendant work. She would soon get bored doing nothing.

Mrs Mercier began to ask Randal about Venice, and he promised to show her some of the photographs he had taken of Laura there. 'I'll have them developed right away,' he said.

His mother talked nostalgically about the city, then asked Laura's opinion of it, and Laura answered enthusiastically. After half an hour Randal looked at his watch.

'An early night tonight, I think,' he said. 'I've got to get up for work tomorrow; there'll be a mountain of work waiting for me.'

'I'm sure it's done you good to get away,' said Mrs Mercier. 'You work too hard.'

They said goodnight and went up to their suite. Laura stood in the white and gold bedroom, yawning. The flight followed by the nervous tension of their first evening in the house had made her sleepy. Randal watched her, his dark face expressionless.

'Are you hinting that you want to go straight to sleep?' he enquired sardonically.

She flushed and looked at him nervously, wondering how to answer. He sounded angry. Did he want to make love to her? She had somehow thought he would not do so tonight.

He stalked past her into the bathroom and slammed the door. She began to undress slowly, feeling utterly miserable. She slid into a white lace negligée and tied it at the waist with a wide pink satin belt just as Randal emerged, his dark hair damp, his lean body already clothed in pyjamas. Without a glance at her he walked to the bed. She went into the bathroom to wash. When she returned he had put out the light and was lying silent in the bed. She untied her belt, slid out of the negligée and got into bed beside him.

Lying in the dark beside him she wondered whether to say goodnight or not. His attitude was bewildering. She could feel the rigidity of his body beside her, but she could not guess what he was thinking.

While she hesitated, cautiously weighing up the pros and cons, her body was slowly relaxing in the warmth of the bed. Sleep crept over her as irresistibly as a summer tide.

She awoke during the night to wonder where she was and stare confusedly at the alien shapes of the furniture in the darkness, then with a leap of memory to realise, hearing the regular sound of breathing beside her.

Cautiously she turned on her side towards Randal. He was lying neatly on his side facing her, his face a pale shimmer in the darkness.

She stared at him intently, trying to make herself believe that he was really her husband and she really was lying here in the spacious suite his parents had given them. Then she thought about Tom, in guilty regret, and about her mother, who had lost her for ever and been forced to engage a housekeeper to run the home and look after her. Laura had actually chosen the woman, a local widow whom Mrs Knight had suggested, and had been favourably impressed by Mrs Grant's easy-going cheerfulness, but she knew her mother would be missing her, and she could not repress a feeling of guilt about that, too.

Her marriage to Randal had solved the problem of her father's weakness in embezzling money from his firm, but it had not solved some other problems.

Indeed, it had created others she could never have foreseen in the beginning.

Shaking off that thought, she leaned over to pick up her watch and peer at the time. Four o'clock. She sighed. Why had sleep become evasive suddenly? Her body was warm and slack but her mind was peculiarly active. Staring at the window, she wondered how long it would be before dawn. In a way, her marriage was a long night, filled with a breathless excitement, but trapping her in confusion, darkness and bewilderment.

She twisted over on to her side again and had a shock when she met Randal's glittering eyes in the darkness.

'I'm sorry,' she stammered. 'Did I wake you?'

'Yes,' he said harshly. 'And now you must take the consequences.'

For a moment she did not understand what he meant, but as the hard body moved, she gasped in violent protest. 'No, don't ... I don't want to ...'

'Too bad,' Randal said savagely. 'Because I want to. You woke me up from a particularly pleasant dream ...'

'Let me go!' she whispered furiously, twisting out from under him.

His hands dragged her back, ripping the flimsy chiffon. 'Oh ...' she cried angrily, 'look what you've done!'

Without a word he tore the nightdress away from her and flung it to the floor, holding her down with the weight of his body, one hand tangled in her hair so that she could not move without pain. She moaned protestingly as his mouth forced her lips apart. He was as brutal as he had been once before, when he kissed her in his car.

As he freed her hair and ran his hands down over her body, his breath coming faster, she pushed at his chest, struggling violently, hitting him in the face, her nails scratching at him.

He drew back his head out of her reach, his face a pale triangle beneath the dark cap of his hair. 'Stop fighting me, damn you!'

'You're hurting me,' she panted, still struggling. 'I told you, I don't want to tonight ...'

'I want to hurt you,' he said in harsh honesty. 'Do you think I don't know why you can't sleep? Your mind's somewhere else, isn't it? Well, your body can't escape me.'

In the past when he made love to her there had been warmth and delight in the way he touched her, his hands and mouth coaxing and seductive, his whole being concentrated on bringing her, as well as himself, to the crest of physical pleasure. But she knew she would get no tenderness tonight, no sweet teasing and no gentleness.

'I hate you!' she sobbed at him, helpless in the force of his silent possession.

He bruised her smooth skin, violated her body and mind, the cruelty of his passion searing, making her as tense as a violin string. She never ceased to resist him, giving no concessions, but when he was spent and rolled away in silence to turn his back on her, tears ran down her face as she lay awake, hating him. Was this to be the pattern of their lives together? She fell asleep in a grey daylight and slept on until late in the morning. When she did wake up it was to find Randal gone.

'He's always at the office by nine,' his mother told her, smiling indulgently as Laura ate rolls and Italian cherry jam with her coffee.

'I'm so sorry I overslept,' Laura apologised again.

'My dear, you must do exactly as you wish,' Mrs Mercier said gently. 'Will you lunch here today? Randal said he wouldn't be home for lunch.'

'If you don't mind I think I should visit my parents today,' Laura said.

'Of course—I understand. You must be worried about your mother. I hope you find her well.'

Laura stood up and Mrs Mercier asked her how she was going to get to her parents' house. 'Take the car,' she urged.

'I don't drive,' Laura admitted.

'That doesn't matter. The chauffeur will take you— I'll ring for him now. But you must have driving lessons right away. You ought to know how to drive a car.'

At least it would fill in the time, Laura thought, as she drove across London in the chauffeur-driven limousine. The car halted outside her home and she told him to pick her up at four o'clock. That would give her plenty of time with her mother, she decided.

Mrs Hallam looked remarkably well and happy when she came to meet Laura in the hall.

Laura kissed her and laughed. 'I can see Mrs Grant is looking after you, anyway. I think you've put on a pound or two! She must be a good cook.'

'Oh, she is,' Mrs Hallam agreed. 'We get on very well together. I think it's going to work out very well.'

Mrs Grant came out of the kitchen to greet Laura, asking if she would be there for lunch.

'If it isn't too much trouble for you,' Laura said.

'No trouble at all,' said Mrs Grant. 'I thought you might be over today, so I made more than usual.' She smiled. 'I hope you like gammon steaks? I've made a white sauce with them.'

'It sounds delicious,' smiled Laura.

She sat talking to her mother, telling her about Venice and carefully evading any more private discussions, until the lunch was ready. The meal was well cooked and nicely served. Laura could tell by the easy conversation between her mother and Mrs Grant that they were already friends. She was relieved, yet vaguely regretful, since she had been so necessary to her mother for years and now she felt faintly displaced.

Afterwards they sat together in the sitting-room, drinking coffee and talking quietly, while the room filled with the strange brightness of a spring afternoon. A bowl of blue hyacinth on the window sill released a cloud of sweet fragrance into the warm air. Mrs Hallam leaned back, smiling, watching her daughter's face as she described the Venetian palaces and their gold reflections in the canals.

She put no direct questions, but unknowingly Laura hardly framed a sentence which did not contain the name Randal. 'Randal said ... Randal took me ... Randal and I ...' His name was constantly on her lips, and every time she said it her eyes glowed with unconscious passion.

Mrs Hallam was contented. She was too shrewd to face Laura with the blunt question: 'Are you happy?'

She saw shadows in Laura's green eyes from time to

time, but that Randal was utterly important to her daughter was obvious. All marriage was a matter of compromise, she thought. Human beings are not perfect. They have to learn to live together, to accommodate themselves to another living personality. All that mattered was that they loved each other. The rest would come in time.

Had she known Laura's secret thoughts she might not have been so optimistic. Talking cheerfully, Laura could not repress an inward feeling of alarm and anxiety. Last night had been a nightmare. What would the approaching night bring? Another similar experience?

CHAPTER NINE

At three-thirty she glanced at her watch and sighed. 'I have to go at four,' she explained. She did not want to leave the warm security of her old home. All the luxury and elegance of the Mercier house seemed remote and alien to her at this moment. It was here that she belonged, among the quiet domestic possessions her parents had built up over the years: the small gold clock with its balance swinging round and round, the blue and white porcelain clown they had bought twenty years ago in Paris, the slender red glass vase which always held a single flower, today a narcissus, the white fragility of the flower trembling whenever a door opened and a draught blew past it. These familiar objects made her heart ache suddenly.

Randal was a stranger; a dark, exciting, dangerous stranger who had swept her off her feet and out into strange currents.

The sharp ring of the door bell made her jump. The chauffeur was early, she thought, looking around the room for a last reassuring glimpse of her childhood.

Then the door opened and Tom came in, his face seeming thinner, his hair warm and ruffled, his eyes alight with a smile as he set eyes on her.

'Hallo, stranger,' he said lightly, but beneath the light tone she heard deeper emotions which made her wince.

'How was Venice?' he asked. 'I saw your card. Was the weather good?'

Laura had sent her parents a card during the first week. Randal had watched her write it, leaning over her shoulder to read her words.

She had, in fact, bought a card to send to Tom, but somehow Randal's watchful eyes had made it impossible for her to write the card, so she had pretended she had bought it for someone else. At the time she had suspected Randal was acting deliberately, aware that she had it in mind to send Tom a card and determined that she should not do so. His dog-in-the-manger attitude irritated her. He had told her so firmly that he did not care where she bestowed her heart so long as he could own her body, yet at every turn he made it plain that he resented her affection for Tom. She might have begun to think he was jealous, had he not shown her so plainly in the last two days that he was not in the least in love with her. No man in love, she thought wistfully, could have been so coldly cruel as he had been last night.

He wants to come between me and Tom, but he has no intention of loving me, she thought bitterly, as she talked to Tom about Venice. Tom looked down at Mrs Hallam with a smile.

'Your mother is looking well, isn't she? I've been keeping my eye on her for you. I think Mrs Grant is going to be a treasure.'

Laura was slightly jealous, feeling that even here, where she had once been essential, she was not needed. The whole world seemed cold to her as she noticed the time again. Four o'clock ... any minute now the chauffeur would be knocking at the door.

'I must go,' said Tom. 'I've got some calls to make. Walk me to the door, Laurie.'

She walked with him into the hall. He carefully closed

the door of the sitting-room, then turned to face her, his eyes serious.

'Is everything all right, Laurie?'

Her face was wary. 'Of course,' she said brightly.

His eyes searched her small, pale face. 'You were smiling a good deal in there, but I had the feeling you were hiding something. Are you sure something isn't wrong?'

Her lower lip trembled. His concerned affection made her suddenly weak. She put a shaking hand to her eyes and leaned against his shoulder, and his arm came round her, holding her tight. She felt the muscles in his arm contract and heard his breath draw in sharply as he touched her.

'Laurie,' he said huskily. 'My darling, don't cry ...'

'I'm sorry,' she said, tears coursing down her face. 'I'm sorry ...' She sniffed, rubbing her eyes in a childish effort to stop the tears.

Tom groaned and pulled her head against his chest, stroking her shining hair with an uneven hand.

The door bell rang at that moment, making them both jump violently. While Tom answered it Laura tried to pull herself together, blowing her nose with a handkerchief and pushing back a wayward wisp of hair.

Tom stepped back without speaking. His silence and rigidity made her heart turn over.

Without looking she knew who stood on the doorstep. She walked like a pale ghost towards him, her eyes hidden under their slightly reddened eyelids.

Randal stood aside as she walked past him. She could feel the anger in him like the threat of an elemental storm, but she did not look up. She heard the quiet closing of the front door. It sounded like the end of something and she nearly began to cry again, but she would not cry in front of Randal.

He opened the door of his car and stood back, watching her seat herself, then walked round and got behind the wheel.

The engine raced into life. They slid away from the kerb and shot into the slowly falling dusk.

When she finally glanced at Randal his face was sombre and uncommunicative. She cleared her throat nervously. She could not bear this silence a moment longer.

'You got away from the office early?'

As if she had pressed a button he turned on her savagely. 'Yes, I had the foolish idea that we might do something this afternoon—go for a drive in the country, maybe. I came home and found you gone.'

'I told you I was going to see my mother,' she said quietly.

He laughed, his dark face derisive. 'Your mother! You mean you'd run off to find your Beloved Physician, our noble, pure-minded friend who can hardly keep his hands off you, the sly, hypocritical bastard!'

She went white, staring at him. 'Tom has never...'

'What was going on when I arrived, then?' he jumped in furiously. 'Or did I imagine I saw your outlines through the glass in the front door ... so tenderly entwined, his arm round your neck and your head on his shoulder. A pity I came along so inopportunely, wasn't it? Another moment and he would have been kissing the tears away. How you would have enjoyed that, my darling. You couldn't wait twenty-four hours to get back to him, could you?'

Remembering last night she was dazed. He was baffling, a near schizophrenic, never the same person for twenty-four hours. How could she ever understand him?

'You ... you said you didn't care if I loved him,' she whispered nervously, terrified of him in this mood.

The car shot forward and tore along the centre of the road, swerving in and out of the traffic, eating the miles at a speed which she dared not contemplate.

Suddenly Randal braked, sending her tumbling forward in her seat, held only by her seat-belt. Breathless, she looked outside and saw that they were back at the Mercier house. The porch light glowed softly over the steps and some of the windows were outlined in bright light, but the street was quiet and deserted.

Randal looked at her dangerously, his colour high, his eyes as sharp and bright as steel daggers.

'When I bought you I bought all of you. I don't want half a wife. I will not leave here in the morning not knowing if you're with him or not while I'm at work.' His hand seized her wrist, tightening cruelly on her until she cried out softly against the pain. 'Am I making myself clear? I can't stop you loving the bastard—I wouldn't even try. But I will not have you meeting him in secret. From now on, you're never to see him again. Never.' His eyes bored into her. 'Do you get that? Never!'

Somehow Laura got through that long evening without breaking down. She ate her dinner, talked quietly to Mr and Mrs Mercier, played backgammon with Mr Mercier and was mercilessly thrashed, and then watched an old film on television until nearly midnight. She was tired long before the film ended, but she was dreading the night so much that she could not bring herself to go upstairs.

When she had switched the television off she sat staring at the blank screen, crouched on a stool, like a child being punished for some misdemeanour.

The door opened and she visibly jumped, looking round at Randal with eyes full of fear and misery.

He strode over to her and pulled her up. 'Come to bed,' he said grimly. He was already in pyjamas and dressing-gown, having gone up an hour ago.

Laura washed and changed into her nightdress with trembling fingers. Randal had laid it out on the bed for her, choosing, quite deliberately she was certain, one so brief and revealing that she was almost naked. She hesitated at the bathroom door, shivering with nerves.

'For God's sake come to bed,' he snapped from the bedroom.

Snapping off the light, she silently crossed the room and climbed into bed beside him, watched every inch of the way by eyes that seemed to her to be full of hatred.

He reached up and pulled the light cord, and the room plunged into darkness.

Laura lay there, shuddering, expecting him to turn to her and begin making love to her as savagely as he had last night.

When he did move her body jerked convulsively. Randal's voice bit through the darkness.

'Go to sleep, Laura. You can stop quivering like a hypnotised rabbit. I don't want you tonight—I couldn't touch you if I tried.'

Relief and bitterness made her throat clench with salty tears. She turned on to her side without a word and wept silently, her tears soaking into her pillow. Gradually she stopped crying and went to sleep, and when she woke up it was morning and Randal had gone.

Mrs Mercier suggested over breakfast that she might like to cook Randal a meal in their suite that evening.

'Not that I'm not very happy to have you both downstairs, but I'm sure you're dying to try out your kitchen.'

Laura thanked her, smiling somehow, and later went out to shop for food to cook. She managed to while away the morning doing this and returned back to the house for lunch, then spent the afternoon in their suite, preparing the meal and enjoying the feel of being quite alone for the first time in weeks.

At six o'clock the telephone rang in their sitting-room, making her jump. She answered it nervously.

'I shan't be home for dinner tonight, you'll be relieved to hear,' Randal said crisply. 'I'm dining out.'

'Oh,' she said blankly.

'You can tell my mother I have to see an American exporter,' he added.

'Yes,' she said.

There was a pause. 'What did you do today?' he asked her abruptly.

'Just some shopping,' she said, adding bitterly, 'I didn't see Tom, if that's what you mean.'

He hung up with a crash which half deafened her. She went into the little kitchenette and looked at the food all carefully prepared for cooking. Anger burned at the back of her eyes. She could have screamed.

Instead she went downstairs and told Mrs Mercier that Randal would not be home. His mother was wry and unsurprised. 'He works too hard. You must teach him better habits, my dear. Never mind, it means we shall have you to ourselves tonight. I hope you won't get bored with us.'

'I'm sure I shan't,' said Laura. 'But if it's inconvenient I do have that food upstairs, you know.'

'Unless you prefer to eat alone, we shall be delighted

for you to eat with us,' Mrs Mercier said kindly. 'I warn you, Yves is going to ask you to play backgammon with him, though. Randal always beats him. He's a born gambler, my son, I'm afraid. He likes the danger and the excitement, and he takes appalling risks. I was always afraid he would kill himself in those fast cars he loves, but luckily he does have enormous control.'

I haven't noticed, Laura thought bitterly.

She went back up to her own rooms at eleven o'clock. Randal had not returned. She was in bed reading when the door finally opened and he looked at her across the room. Dark-faced, unsmiling, he nodded.

'Not asleep yet? And I was sure I'd find you dead to the world.' The words had a sardonic ring which she ignored.

She put down her book and turned over on to her side, pulling the bedclothes up over her shoulders. Ten minutes later he got into bed and settled down to sleep. She felt as though there were a wall between them, high and forbidding. All the passion and laughter had vanished from their relationship. Randal had turned into a terrifying stranger who hated her.

As the days went by she began to think she would never again lie in his arms. They shared the suite, they shared a bed, but his eyes never seemed to meet hers and if they brushed against each other, moving around the rooms, he gave no sign of noticing her.

Sometimes she did not see him for several days. He would come home from the office after midnight and be gone before she woke up. The only sign that he had slept in the same bed would be the deep indentation of his head in the pillow and a dark hair or two straying on the white sheets.

She visited her mother from time to time, rarely staying long for fear of meeting Tom. Although she had not given her word to Randal she felt impelled to do as he insisted and avoid Tom.

She spent her evenings with the Mercier family, sometimes talking to his sisters, who were occasional visitors; sometimes playing chess or backgammon with Yves Mercier, sometimes watching television or listening to records.

Six weeks after they had returned from Venice she realised she was pregnant. The idea came as a shock so profound that she could not quite believe it at first. Randal had become so much a hostile stranger that it was as if she had become pregnant by another man.

The thought of telling Randal was intolerable. She brooded about it for some days before she knew she had to talk to someone. She could hardly tell her mother. Mrs Hallam would be delighted with the news, and Laura had concealed from her any vestige of the truth about her marriage, so a confidence now might bring on a fatal heart attack. She dared not talk to Mrs Mercier, either. She was, after all, Randal's mother, and although clear-sighted about him she was quite obviously deeply attached to him, too.

Laura knew that only one person could begin to understand how she felt. But how could she see Tom without breaking her unspoken oath to Randal? Although she had never promised not to see Tom again, she knew her silence had been a form of consent.

At the beginning of May the weather turned unseasonably sultry. Getting up one hot morning, Laura felt violently sick. She staggered back to bed and lay there, shivering. Was she ill? she thought. Then it dawned on her. She was not experienced enough to recognise the symptoms of morning sickness at first, but she had heard of it vaguely and guessed that this was only the beginning of a process she had to learn more about.

She had a choice. She could either go to her own doctor and get sensible advice, or she could talk to Tom. She hesitated for two more days, torn between the desire to talk to him and a feeling that she owed her loyalty to Randal, despite his cruelty.

That afternoon she went out shopping in London and on an impulse suddenly took a taxi to her home. Her mother was surprised but pleased to see her.

Just as Laura was meaning to leave, Tom arrived and looked at her in startled surprise. 'How are you? I don't seem to have seen you for weeks.'

She flushed slightly, wondering if he guessed the reason. 'Yes, we seem to have missed each other lately,' she said lightly. 'Just one of those things. Are you as busy as ever, Tom?'

'Busier, if anything,' he said. His face sobered. 'You know my mother has died?'

She was shocked. 'No, I didn't,' she said with sadness. She had been fond of Tom's mother.

'I forgot to tell you,' said Mrs Hallam in self-reproach. 'You didn't come last week and when you did pop over it was only for such a short time, I suppose it escaped my mind . . .'

'The funeral was two days ago,' Tom said. He looked paler than ever, his eyes lined with weariness. 'Dad was a bit shaken. He's gone off to visit his sister in Scarborough for a break. He's thinking of retiring now. He'd been considering it for a year, and putting it off, so now he feels a little guilty. Mum wanted him to retire.'

'I'm so sorry, Tom,' Laura said quietly. She knew how close he was to both his parents.

A little later Tom asked, 'What time are you leaving? Is your husband picking you up?'

'No,' she said flatly. 'I came by taxi. I suppose I'll have to go back the same way. Randal is going out to a business dinner tonight.'

'Why not let me drive you home?' Tom offered. 'I'm off duty now.'

She hesitated, then accepted gratefully. Her mother looked at her anxiously, but said nothing.

In the car Tom looked at her, his hands flat on the wheel. 'You look like death, Laurie. What are you doing about dinner tonight? Why not have dinner with me? I want to talk to you.'

She was not sure how to reply, but her own need to talk to someone overcame her doubts. 'If you stop at a callbox I can ring the family,' she said.

Mrs Mercier sounded surprised when she told her she would be having dinner with a friend, but Laura did not wait long enough for her to ask any quesions.

Tom drove her to a quiet riverside restaurant and they sat at a table out on the flat roof overlooking the river Thames. Along the shore the street lamps gleamed through a faint summer mist. The London skyline stretched away, uneven and romantic, spires and office blocks fading into the distance. The dome of St Paul's shone with an unearthly light and at the other end of the river's curve the Gothic outline of Big Ben ate into the sky.

Tom leaned his hands on the table and looked at her seriously. 'What's wrong, Laurie? Don't pretend that nothing is ... I know you too well.' A smile of ironic sadness touched his mouth. 'I've known you all your life, remember.'

Her lids trembled. 'Oh, Tom, it's all so mixed up. I don't know where to begin ...'

'One usually begins at the beginning,' Tom prompted gently, watching her face. 'In the long run it saves time.'

Haltingly she began to tell him about her first meeting with Randal, about his pursuit and her flight, about her father's embezzlement and Randal's terms for not prosecuting.

'So that's why you married him,' Tom said grimly. 'The swine! He blackmailed you into it.'

Her white face quivered.

'Go on,' Tom urged, reaching out to take her hands between his own, his warmth gently comforting her.

She began to talk about the honeymoon, lightly passing over the intimate details but giving him enough information for his face to stiffen.

'Now,' she ended faintly, 'Now we seem to be total strangers. He's tired of me already. He regrets having married me, and I think he blames me for having done it. I should have been his mistress, not his wife. That was what he really wanted.'

Tom was very pale. 'Give him his divorce,' he urged her angrily. 'You mustn't stay with him if things are like that, Laurie. I thought ...' He bit off his words and she looked at him enquiringly.

'You thought what, Tom?'

He grimaced. 'I thought when you married Mercier you were going to be safe and cherished for the rest of your life, but instead you've been caught in a trap. You must leave him, darling. Don't waste your life trying to preserve a marriage that's never really existed. Break free now.'

'I can't, Tom,' she murmured miserably. 'I'm expecting his child.'

Tom's face tightened as though he had been struck. He stared at her. 'Are you sure?'

'I think so,' she confessed, telling him about her morning sickness and other symptoms.

'You must see a doctor right away,' Tom said abruptly. 'You aren't very strong, Laurie. Pregnancy isn't going to be easy for you. You're so slight and finely made ...'

'Tom, I thought ...' She paused, biting her lip. Then she said rapidly, 'I want you to be my doctor. I couldn't bear to have anyone else.'

'No!' He spoke harshly, almost angrily, his eyes full of a baffling emotion.

'But, Tom ...' she pleaded, her lips trembling, 'I need you now. I need to have someone I can trust and feel safe with ...'

'For God's sake, Laurie,' he burst out, 'you must know why I can't!'

'Oh, I know Randal will be angry,' she said persuasively. 'But surely I have the right to choose my own doctor, and he can hardly suspect me of sleeping with you when I'm pregnant!'

Tom's face flamed. 'Sleeping with me!'

She blushed. 'I'm afraid that's what he suspects,' she admitted unevenly. 'He made me swear never to see you again.'

'So that's why you've avoided me lately,' he said. 'I thought there was a reason behind your oddly timed visits. You always came when you knew I wouldn't be calling, didn't you?'

'I'm sorry, Tom,' she said, her hand curling inside his to rub against his palm comfortingly. 'But now I'm pregnant Randal will have to put up with it.'

'It's out of the question for me to attend you,' Tom said heavily.

'But why?' she begged, bewildered.

He stood up and beckoned the waiter, paid the bill and took her arm to walk back to his car. In the car he drove silently, frowning out of the window, his thoughts clearly preoccupied.

Drawing up outside the Mercier house, he looked up at it with a hostile expression. 'So this is where you live now.'

'Tom, tell me why you refuse to look after me and my baby?' she asked pleadingly.

He sighed deeply, then turned towards her. 'I shan't be here, Laurie.'

'Not here?' For a few seconds she stared, unable to take in his meaning. 'Why not?'

'I'm leaving England,' he said. 'Probably in three months' time. I shall have to work out my notice and sell up.'

'Tom!' She was distracted, unable to believe he meant it. 'Why? Where are you going?'

'For a long time I've had a dream of working in India,' he said. 'I'm useful in the East End. The people need a doctor and I like to be able to help them. But if I'm not there, someone else will do my job. I'm not essential. In the under-developed countries of the world there's not the same pool of medical expertise, though. Doctors aren't to be found on every tree.'

'India?' She shuddered. 'So far away? But for how long? A year? Two?'

'For good, Laurie,' he said gently, turning to look at her with loving eyes. 'I won't be coming back. I feel I'm needed out there as I never have been at home. I may not stay in India. I shall be working with the World Health Organisation. They say they'll send me wherever doctors are needed. Africa, Asia, South America ... I'll be moving around a lot from now on, but always where I'm desperately needed.'

Laura stared at him in utter consternation, refusing to believe that he was going away for ever, that she might never see him again.

'You can't!' she wailed like a deserted child, reaching out to him with pleading hands.

He took her hands slowly and looked at her, his face taut. Suddenly he bent his head and buried his mouth against her palm, kissing first one then the other.

Laurie froze incredulously. Against her hands Tom whispered huskily, 'I love you, Laurie—I always have, I always will. But I always knew I mustn't marry you. You could never survive the life I shall have to lead. Living in tents in burning deserts, or in the ruins of a city after an earthquake, exposed to cholera, typhoid, smallpox ... I couldn't risk your life like that. For a long time I fought against myself. I wanted to marry you, look after you. But there are some things which are stronger than love, darling, and one of them is a sense of vocation. All my life I've wanted to do what I'm going to do now. Faced with the choice of having you or spending my life looking after desperate, helpless people, I had to choose those who needed me most. I knew you would survive without me, but what about those others, the ones who would die without a doctor's help? You do see, don't you, my darling?'

'Oh, Tom,' she said faintly. 'I never guessed that was why ... sometimes I thought you loved me, then you would shut me out.'

'I had to,' he said in an agonised voice. 'What else could I honourably do? Do you think I didn't see that you were turning towards me? You were still so young, but I was tempted beyond endurance at times ...' He laughed in sudden bitterness. 'And to think that I was so relieved and reassured when you married Mercier! I thought it solved my problem for good. I was sick with jealousy, but I couldn't be selfish enough to grudge you your happiness. I was even grateful to him for giving you all the things you needed, the security, the protection, the love ...'

Her head was swimming. She stared at him dazedly, seeing him dissolve strangely. 'Oh, Tom,' she said again, and slid down on to his knees in a dead faint.

Tom exclaimed in horror, lifting her. She lay across his shoulder, as limp as a rag, her upturned face completely white. He looked at the house urgently. It was dark, no sign of a light anywhere. Propping her up against the seat, he searched in her handbag and found a keyring. He went to the front door and tried several keys until he found the right one. Leaving the door ajar, he walked back to the car. Laura was stirring slightly, her lips parted in gasping breath.

He swung her up into his arms and carried her easily up the steps into the house. Remembering her description of their suite, he then began to climb the stairs. He shouldered his way through the door leading to the suite and pushed open the first door he came to in the corridor beyond.

The room lay in darkness, but he could just make out

the shape of a bed. He carried her towards it and laid her down gently, beginning to undo her coat to let her breathe more easily.

Suddenly the light was switched on and he whirled round, his face flushing darkly.

Randal Mercier stood at the door, his face black with rage, his grey eyes glittering dangerously.

'Get your lecherous hands off my wife, you bastard,' he said viciously. 'I'll break your damned neck in three separate places for this!'

Just then Laura stirred, moaning faintly, and Tom turned back to her, his expression anxious. 'It's all right, my darling,' he said gently. 'Lie still ...'

Randal shot across the room and clamped a hand on his shoulder, pulling him round. The next moment he had knocked Tom across the room, his fist connecting with a jarring thud. Tom fell with a crash and Laura sat up, swaying, her white face totally confused.

She looked at Randal in bewilderment, then saw Tom, scrambling to his feet, blood running from the corner of his mouth. A low cry of terror escaped her.

'No, Randal, please no,' she whispered, trembling.

Randal looked at Tom, his mouth reined in tight. 'Get out,' he said between his clenched teeth.

'There's something you must understand ...' Tom began.

'Get out before I throw you out!' Randal bit off.

'But I must tell you first ...' Tom said, then broke off as Randal looked at him savagely, his eyes leaping with angry fire.

'Don't you understand English? She's mine now. She always will be. I will never let her go. Is that quite clear? If you get in my way again I'll kill you!'

'If you hurt her again I'll kill you,' Tom said hoarsely.

Randal's face went white. He looked at Laura contemptuously. 'Did you go to him for comfort, my dear sweet loyal little wife? I suppose you tell yourself that I drove you into his arms?'

Laura looked piteously at Tom. 'You'd better go, Tom —please. Go now.'

He hesitated. 'Are you sure you'll be all right? This madman may not be responsible for his actions.'

'I certainly won't be if you don't get out of my house,' Randal promised him starkly.

Tom looked at him scornfully. 'Do you think I'm afraid of anything you might do to me? All I care about is what you may do to her.'

'I won't lay a finger on her,' Randal said darkly. 'I doubt if I shall ever be able to look at her again.'

Tom hesitated. Laura whispered again, 'Please, Tom, go ...'

Tom sighed, shrugged and walked across the room to the door. Standing there, he turned and looked at her, his face filled with love and concern.

'If you need me you know where to find me.'

She nodded wearily. 'Thank you, Tom.'

He nodded and went out. In the long silence that succeeded his departure she heard the front door close behind him and then the sound of his car driving away.

Randal was watching her grimly. She forced herself to look at him, her eyes wide and apprehensive. What was he going to do now?

'You'd better go to bed,' he said abruptly after what seemed an eternity. 'You look half dead.'

He turned on his heel and went out, slamming the door behind him. Laura sat there for a long while, shivering, then got up with an effort and got ready for bed.

As she pulled back the sheets, her limbs shaking with cold, she found tears pouring down her face. She lay in the bed, unable to move, weeping without even knowing why, consumed with desolation.

The door opened, and through the rain of tears she saw Randal's face. His eyes stared at her mercilessly.

Making an effort that nearly drained her last strength, she brushed a hand across her eyes to dry the tears. The childish gesture seemed to drive Randal mad. He moved fast across the room and lifted her by the shoulders, shaking her violently, her head flopping like that of a rag doll.

Suddenly his hands stopped moving. She hung between them limply, staring at him with wet eyes.

'Oh, hell!' he said thickly. 'What's the point? Very well, Laura, you win. I'll give you a divorce whenever you like.'

CHAPTER TEN

SHE was too shocked to speak for a moment. A wave of icy coldness crept over her as his words sank in, and she swallowed a half sob. But after all, hadn't she been expecting this? She had suspected he was tired of her, and this proved it. Wearily, she said, 'You want a divorce...'

He had been watching her in that old, familiar way, a fox at a hedgerow watching for rabbits; wary, secretive, intent. At her words a muscle jerked in his hard brown cheek. His mouth thinned. He released her shoulders, turned and walked across the room. Laura followed his movements with her eyes, watching as he picked up her hairbrush from the dressing-table and fiddled with it, pulling a stray silver-gilt strand of hair from it. Randal laid the hair across his palm and stared at with a fixed, blank expression.

Without looking round he asked her suddenly, 'May I ask you something?'

'Yes?' she whispered.

'If I give you a divorce will you marry Tom Nicol?'

She flushed. 'No.'

He spun round. 'No?' The grey eyes were narrowed in close scrutiny of her. 'Are you asking me to believe he isn't in love with you? You've told me often enough that you love him. I thought he was the stumbling block, that he didn't love you. After tonight I'm damned sure he does.'

She sat on the edge of the bed, her slight body drooping in defeat, her head lowered as though the weight of it was too much for her slender neck. Staring at the floor, she said quietly, 'Yes, he loves me ... in his way ...'

'What's that supposed to mean?' he demanded in sudden savagery.

She raised her eyes at his tone, trembling. 'I don't know ... I suppose I mean he loves me, but not enough ...'

'Not enough for you?' he asked quickly.

'Not enough for either of us,' she expanded, struggling to explain it to him. 'He wants to work in the underdeveloped countries. He's going to work for the World Health Organisation, and he doesn't think that sort of life would be possible for me. He feels it would be too hard.' She smiled mirthlessly. 'Tom thinks I'm delicate.'

'At least he has sense enough to realise that,' said Randal. He slammed her hairbrush down on the dressing-table. 'I can understand why he decided to go out there to work after you married me, but if you were free again wouldn't he change his plans? Stay here and marry you?'

'Is that what you want me to say?' she asked flatly. 'Will it make it easier for you?'

'Easier for me?' His voice was charged with rage. He took a step towards her, then halted, his hands clenched at his sides, breathing hard. Taking a long, deep breath, he said more coolly, 'Let's leave my feelings out of this for a moment. I want to be sure about yours first. I'll ask you again. If I divorce you, will you marry Tom Nicol?'

'I've told you ... no!'

He pushed his hands into his pockets. 'So where does that leave us? Do I take it you don't want a divorce?'

She looked at him uncertainly. 'Do you?' Her voice trembled on the question.

'No,' he said starkly.

She raised her eyes to his face again, in a quick searching glance, as if unable to believe him. 'Are you sure? I thought ...' Her voice broke suddenly and she looked down, biting her lip, and struggling with tears.

'Thought what?' he asked sharply.

'That ... you were ... tired of me,' she stammered.

'Tired of you?' His voice held the resonance of a groan. Her eyes flew to his face. Their eyes locked in a long duel. Hers fell, her face suffused suddenly with a delicate pink as she read the expression in his gaze. She was trembling, overwhelmed by unbelievable hope. Randal took a step nearer, then another. The long, powerful fingers lifted her chin. She could not look at him, shaken to her depths.

'Look at me,' he ordered softly. 'I want to see what you're hiding from me.'

Reluctantly the long, bright lashes lifted and she looked at him guardedly, still afraid to reveal her love, still hiding how she felt. Even now, with this new vision of happiness shining before her, she dared not expose herself to his mockery. He might still be playing some elaborate game.

His eyes searched her face, probing the green brightness of her eyes, lingering on the trembling softness of her pink mouth, the delicate curve of her tear-stained cheek.

Deliberately, choosing his words with care, he said, 'When we first married I hoped every night that I would hear your voice telling me you loved me.' He smiled wryly. 'As you know, I never did. You know the old saying ... hope deferred maketh the heart sick. After a while I couldn't bear to make love to you at all.'

Laura watched his face incredulously, trying to decide

whether he meant what he said. Could he possibly be hinting that he loved her? Or hadn't she understood him?

'Are you saying ... do you mean ... you're in love with me?' she asked faintly.

His face altered, and the long mouth smiled cynically. 'Quite desperately, my dear,' he drawled in that voice she hated, that mocking, tormenting voice he had often used before to hurt and humiliate her. She flushed and turned away. So after all it had been another of his elaborate charades designed to trap her into an admission of love for him, an admission which would finally make her entirely his possession, owned body and soul. Randal had a strong streak of possessiveness.

His hands caught at her, jerking her back to face him. She looked up in angry protest, words of defiance on her lips. He was incredibly pale, his face revealed as she had never seen it before, the grey eyes leaping with fire, the hard mouth tensely controlled, as though he only just suppressed some fierce, catastrophic emotion.

'Did you hear what I said?' he demanded hoarsely. 'I love you!'

She stared at him in blank disbelief. 'I don't believe you.'

'Don't you, by God?' he said thickly. He bent her backwards until she lay on the bed, leaning over her, his eyes holding hers, his mouth poised above her. 'Why else do you think I was ready to divorce you? Have you any idea what that offer cost me? The thought of losing you ... of you in another man's arms ... was driving me insane, but I couldn't stand the way we were another second. I couldn't bear to see you suffer. Your eyes looked like the eyes of a trapped animal ...'

Her heart was racing violently as she listened. The incredible hope was becoming real right before her eyes. She was beginning to believe him; the agony in his voice was too convincing. Happiness made her light-headed. The gold-tipped lashes stirred on her cheek, hiding her eyes from him, and a smile began to curve her mouth. She looked up at him through her lashes, her lips parting in provocative invitation.

'Stop talking and kiss me, Randal,' she murmured.

She heard his sharp-drawn breath, then his mouth slowly came down towards hers. When it was almost touching her, she moaned huskily, passion flaming deep inside her, winding her arms around his neck to pull him closer, her lips parting in hungry response as their mouths met. The kiss seemed endless, as if he could not satisfy his need of her, his fingers wound in her hair, forcing back her head.

Just as she thought she would die of suffocation, he lifted her in his arms and moved her to the centre of the bed. She watched dreamily as he flung his jacket to the floor and began to unbutton his shirt. It was so long since he had made love to her. She was dizzy, her body singing with desire.

He lay down beside her and looked deep into her eyes, their feelings no longer cloaked from him. 'Oh, God, I love you,' he said hoarsely. 'You intoxicate me.'

She laid her palms against the hard wall of his chest, running her hands softly up to his shoulders, the palms gripping him. Her mouth was dry with an intolerable excitement. 'Darling,' she whispered. 'Oh, darling ...'

He undid her blouse and buried his face between her breasts, groaning softly.

She was trembling, impatient for him, her pulses hammering. The room seemed to be spinning around her. She took his dark head between her hands and raised it, groaning. 'Randal ... Randal ...'

Her voice died away under the blaze of his eyes, and a slow spiral of exquisite pleasure built up inside her. Their surroundings melted away. The only reality was their own bodies, caught up in that frenzied ecstasy.

When the room grew solid again the flames which had consumed them both were dying down slowly, leaving the memory of an utter sweetness, a consummation so complete that she was still shaking with it, her ears filled with the sound of Randal's voice splintering into a thousand fragments of agony and pleasure. Now his face was buried against the warm softness of her body and he was trembling convulsively.

Against her shoulder he said quietly, 'I wanted to possess you the first time we met. I took one look at you and I knew I'd die if I couldn't have you. Nothing like it had ever happened to me before and for a while I believed you must feel the same. When I realised you were in love with another man it was too late. I was so crazy about you I would have committed murder to get you.'

'Why didn't you tell me? Why did you say you only wanted my body, not my heart?' she asked in gentle reproach.

He raised his head to smile down at her, the old, half taunting smile. 'I suspected that if you knew how completely I'd lost my head over you, you might use it against me. I knew I had to marry you. I couldn't walk away and leave you; you had to belong to me. But you were in love with Nicol, then. You wouldn't have married me unless I'd blackmailed you into it. For a while I hoped that by being around all the time I could coax you into loving me. Then your father's little time-bomb exploded, and for your sake I had to let him off the hook.' His mouth twisted wryly. 'It was an unscrupulous thing to do, but I was desperate enough to use anything by then.'

'You took a terrible risk, Randal,' she said. 'I might have hated you for the rest of our lives.'

'Do you think I didn't know that?' He was pale suddenly, his eyes filled with pain. 'I gambled on one thing ... the way our mutual chemistry worked.'

She blushed and he laughed at her tenderly, kissing her bare shoulder.

'That was the only hope I had, don't you see? Your eyes might hate me, but your body told me a different story. It puzzled me, but I couldn't resist taking advantage of it. I convinced myself that once I got you into bed I could teach you to love me. It was a long shot, but I had no other choice. I hoped your love for the noble doctor was a schoolgirl crush you'd never outgrown. I thought by teaching you to enjoy making love I would gradually make you fall for me instead ...'

'Which I promptly did,' she said softly.

'Did you?' He leaned over her demandingly. 'You never gave me an inkling. When did you start to love me?'

She shrugged helplessly. 'I don't know. When we first met, perhaps, but I was so used to the idea of loving Tom that I didn't recognise the way I felt about you as love. You made me angry and excited. When you kissed me, my head spun, but I still thought it was just ... what did you call it? Chemistry?'

He laughed mockingly. 'That was your body recognising what your heart refused to see,' he murmured. 'When did you first realise you loved me, then?'

'In Venice,' she said, her eyes closing at the memory.

'After that Party at Antoinette Bell's ...'

'Oh, yes,' he said softly. 'I was very hopeful that night. You looked at me in such an exciting way, your eyes half closed. We were dancing, do you remember?'

'Oh, I remember,' she said. 'I wanted you suddenly ...'

'That was obvious,' he drawled.

Her eyes flew open. She looked at him and laughed. 'You know me better than I know myself,' she admitted. 'I suddenly realised I was jealous of Antoinette Bell.' Her glance accused him. 'I was so sure she'd been your mistress and I found I couldn't bear the idea.'

'Good,' he said, kissing her softly. 'I'm glad I wasn't the only one to feel jealousy—God knows I had enough of it over Tom Nicol. I thought for a moment tonight I was really going to kill him. A red tide seemed to come up over my eyes. I only just stopped myself from breaking his neck.'

'I thought you'd break mine when you shook me like that,' she said with a shiver.

His hand slid over her throat, caressing her. 'I think I actually wanted to kill you at that moment, yes. Then I saw your tear-stained little face and I went icy cold. I couldn't bear to see you so unhappy. I had to let you go.' He sighed. 'Tell me you don't love him any more. I want to hear you say it.'

'I don't love him,' she said huskily. 'I thought I did once, but it was a mirage. The way I feel about you is totally different.' She wound her arms around his neck and kissed his neck, saying passionately, 'I love you, I love you, Randal ...'

His hands came up to hold her closer. 'Entirely and absolutely?'

'Entirely and absolutely,' she repeated deeply.

He lifted her body up until their mouths met. The long kiss drained her and she lay, breathing hard, against him.

For a while they lay in silence. Then Randal said suddenly, 'Nicol is a fool. If he hadn't been obsessed with this idea of working in the under-developed countries, he would have married you, and I would never have met you.'

'What a terrible thought,' she said, shivering. 'I would only have been half alive for the rest of my life. Tom wasn't the man for me. He's a dear, sweet man, but he would never have made me as happy as you have tonight.'

'Yes,' he said soberly. 'There's a great gulf between being moderately contented and rapturously alive. You've taken me to hell and given me all of heaven since I met you, and I wouldn't lose one hour of knowing you even to cancel out the anguish you made me suffer.'

'Did I do that?' She was distressed, clinging to him. 'Darling, I'm sorry ... if I'd only guessed ... weeks ago this could have happened ...'

'I was far too determined to keep my secret from you,' he said with a self-derisive twist of his lips. 'I didn't want you to have the satisfaction of knowing I would have sold my soul to hear you say you loved me.'

'You could have given me a hint,' she said. 'Why were you so cruel to me sometimes? That night after our wedding rehearsal, when you made love to me in the car, you terrified me ...'

'I was gambling my life on marrying a woman who didn't love me,' he said sombrely. 'I was angry and jealous and afraid of losing you. My feelings got out of hand that night. You were hurting me so badly I wanted to hurt you back.'

'Was that why you were so brutal to me that night after we got back from Venice, when I woke you at four in the morning, and you made love to me as if you were raping me?' The pain of the memory still throbbed as she talked about it.

'I was raping you,' he said savagely. 'That was how I felt. I wanted to take you as brutally as I knew how. God, I was miserable, Laura. I thought my gamble had been lost. Although you were so sweet and responsive in bed, you seemed as much in love with Nicol as ever, and I was desperate. We were home and you would be seeing him again. The thought of that made me so jealous I could hardly bear to look at you.'

'If only you'd told me!' she groaned. 'I loved you by then. All that anguish could have been avoided.'

'I wish I had,' he admitted. 'I was a coward. I couldn't have borne it if you'd laughed at me or, even worse, been sorry for me.' He grimaced. 'If it's any consolation to you I didn't enjoy it any more than you did. It was hell on earth, but I didn't seem able to stop myself. I wanted to prove to you and to myself that you belonged to me, and there's only one way a man can show a woman that.'

She stroked his face lovingly. 'Poor darling!' A thought occurred to her and she inspected him in sudden coolness. 'You still haven't told me about Antoinette...'

He laughed wickedly. 'You're like a bulldog once you get your teeth into something, aren't you?'

'Tell me the truth,' she demanded.

'The truth?' He grinned, his eyes glinting. 'Well, Antoinette and I did have a little flirtation once. We might even have gone to bed together if a rather alluring

Italian count hadn't come along at the wrong moment. Antoinette suddenly lost interest and I went home to London. We were still friends—there was no love between us to poison the situation. It was all just a game.'

'Do you still think love is a game?' she demanded teasingly.

His eyes darkened with passion. 'A fatal one,' he murmured.

She sighed. 'How do I know you'll always love me? There have been other women, you can't deny it.'

'I never loved any of them,' he said flatly. 'I made love to them—I won't pretend I didn't. But it meant no more than a moment of light pleasure. And then when I fell heavily it had to be for a girl nearly half my age who was mooning over another man ...' He groaned. 'It was a judgment on me for treating love lightly.'

She thought of the child she was carrying, the baby of whose existence Randal was ignorant. Curling herself against him, she said softly, 'I've got something to tell you ...'

He was suddenly tense. She felt his muscles tighten as though in expectation of pain.

'I'm going to have your baby,' she said softly.

He lay very still for a moment, then he turned on his side to look into her eyes, his face incredulous. 'Are you sure?'

'Absolutely certain,' she said with a little smile.

'My God,' he breathed. 'Why didn't you tell me? When did you realise it?'

'Not long ago,' she said. 'That was why I went to see Tom.'

Randal's face darkened. 'Do you mean he examined you?'

'Don't be jealous, darling,' she soothed. 'Tom refused to take me as a patient. It was silly and thoughtless of me to ask him. That was what triggered off my faint. When I asked him why he wouldn't look after me through my pregnancy he told me ...'

'That he loved you?' Randal asked jealously.

She nodded.

'What do you mean, it triggered off your faint?' he asked in a controlled voice. 'Why should you faint? Unless you're still half in love with him?'

'I'm pregnant, darling,' she said gently. 'I've been sick in the mornings lately and I was feeling very miserable. When Tom said he loved me it suddenly all seemed such a pointless waste. There was I loving you without any hope, and now it seemed Tom loved me in the same tragic, pointless fashion. It made me so unhappy.'

He groaned, kissing her cheek. 'I'll make it up to you, I promise.'

'You already have,' she said, suddenly fired with returning passion.

He moved away slightly, resisting her offered warmth. 'No, we must be careful now,' he said thickly.

She looked at him in bewilderment. 'What do you mean?'

'My sweet little love, you've got to be careful of yourself from now on ... you don't want to lose that baby, do you? For a few months it might be dangerous for us to make love.'

'A few months?' It sounded like eternity. She was indignant. 'By then you won't want me. I'll look like a pumpkin.'

He laughed deep in his throat. 'Oh, I'll want you all right. I adore pumpkins, especially when they've got hair like spun silk and eyes like a cat...' He carefully pulled the bedclothes over her. 'You mustn't catch cold.'

'I shall feel very cold without you for months,' she said reproachfully.

He kissed her lingeringly. 'I'll think of ways to keep you warm, my darling, like telling you I love you, or doing this...' His mouth caressingly explored her throat, making her colour come and go.

She stroked his black hair, her eyelids closing contentedly. The world which had seemed so desolate to her only hours ago was suddenly filled with warmth and joy.

Randal was still there next morning when she woke up, his arms holding her close, his head curving in above her hair. She stretched lazily, so happy she wanted to sing, and at once his hand moved over her smooth flesh in a gentle caress.

'Aren't you going to be late for work?' she asked him, glancing over his shoulder at the clock.

'Who cares?' he said indifferently. 'They'll get along well enough without me there breathing down their necks, and I wanted to stay in bed with you for as long as possible.'

'There were so many mornings when I woke up to find you gone without a word,' she said, remembering sadly.

'That will never happen again,' he promised. 'From now on you'll have to kick me out of your bed to get rid of me.'

She softly bit his shoulder. 'What if I keep you here?'

'Then I'll stay all day,' he said teasingly.

'Won't you get bored?'

His hands moved intimately over her. 'Bored?' His voice deepened. 'You're kidding!'

After a while she felt hungry and nudged him. Sleepily he raised a reluctanct head from her body and drawled, 'Mmm ...?'

'I want my breakfast,' she told him.

'I've told you before—you have a mundane little mind,' he said reprovingly, but he allowed her to get up, watching her from the bed as she moved about getting ready, wandering in and out of the bathroom.

'The view from this bed is fantastic,' he murmured wickedly.

Laura made a face at him. 'Aren't you going to get up?'

'No,' he said. 'Come here.'

She laughed at him and went out of the door. When she got downstairs she found his parents reading the daily newspapers. They looked up in surprise at her. Their breakfast was clearly long finished.

'Good morning,' she said softly, kissing them both.

Mrs Mercier surveyed her with satisfaction. 'You look better this morning. I've been worried about you, Laura. You haven't been looking well lately.'

Yves Mercier cleared his throat, giving his wife a warning glance. She ignored him, her face serious as she went on: 'I meant to speak to Randal about it, but he's so rarely been in ...'

Laura wandered to the sideboard, where a hotplate was keeping the rest of the breakfast hot. She lifted the silver lid and peered at some drying scrambled egg. A toaster and some bread stood beside it. She popped a slice of toast into the toaster, waited until it jumped back up and buttered it thinly, spooning some egg on top of it.

Carrying it back to the table, she sat down opposite her father-in-law and began to eat.

Mrs Mercier coughed. 'I realise it's none of my business,' she said.

'No, it isn't,' her husband interrupted fiercely. 'Leave the child alone. She and Randal must work it out together.'

'She doesn't look well,' Mrs Mercier snapped. 'I'm concerned for her. It isn't natural to look so pale and wan ...'

'It is when you're pregnant,' Laura said casually.

The silence was deafening. Yves Mercier laid down his newspaper carefully. His wife was staring at Laura with a curious expression on her face.

Laura looked up, blushing. 'I've been having morning sickness,' she said shyly. 'It seems to have stopped now.'

Yves Mercier reached across the table and took her hand. He squeezed it tightly, wordless. She smiled at him.

'Does Randal know?' Mrs Mercier demanded. 'Have you told him?'

The door opened and Randal sauntered into the room. 'Has she told me what, Mama?' he asked wickedly.

'Why aren't you at the office?' his father asked him in reproving surprise.

'I'm taking a day off,' Randal said, getting himself some breakfast.

'You're very casual all of a sudden,' growled Mr Mercier, eyeing him crossly.

Randal came to the table, carrying his plate. He paused behind Laura's chair, his eyes on her bent silvery head. Then he quite deliberately lowered his face to brush against her cheek in a gentle caress. 'It isn't every day a man is told he's going to be a father,' he said.

Mr Mercier's face softened. Mrs Mercier let out a long breath of relief. Looking across the table at her Laura wondered just how much she had known of what was happening between herself and Randal. She suspected her mother-in-law had known a good deal.

The butler appeared in the doorway. He coughed and Randal looked round at him impatiently. 'Well?'

'A Doctor Nicol to see Mrs Mercier,' he pronounced, adding, 'The young Mrs Mercier.'

'That must be you, dear,' said her mother-in-law with sharp amusement. 'Unless he means it as a subtle compliment to me.'

The butler's face remained wooden. He withdrew slightly, waiting for his orders.

Randal had laid down his knife and fork and his lean face turned to look at Laura. She saw the jealousy which still lingered in his grey eyes.

'Do you want to see him?' he asked sharply. 'Or shall I see him for you?'

'I'll see him,' she said, getting up.

Randal rose, too. 'Not alone, you won't,' he said in that hard, possessive voice.

She took his hand, smiling at him. 'We'll see him together,' she agreed gently.

Mr Mercier looked at his wife in bewilderment. She was watching her son with a frown that faded as Laura led him from the room, her hand almost swallowed up in the hard grip of his long fingers.

'What's going on?' Yves Mercier asked anxiously.

'Nothing serious,' said his wife, patting his hand. 'I think they're going to be all right.'

Tom was waiting in the hall, his black bag gripped in one hand, his face anxious. His eyes widened as he saw them, hand in hand, Laura's face flushed and smiling.

Randal threw open the morning room door. 'Come in here,' he said brusquely.

Tom faced them, squaring his shoulders. 'I came to make sure Laura was all right,' he said flatly.

'Take a look at her,' Randal said.

Tom grimaced. 'I have.' His voice was uneven. Laura looked at him anxiously. She could not bear to think he was suffering because of her.

'I'm fine, Tom,' she said softly.

'I had to be sure,' he shrugged. He held her eyes. 'I've been awake all night ...'

'So have we,' Randal drawled deliberately.

Tom's face reddened, and Laura looked at Randal indignantly. He was deliberately mocking Tom. He had the grace to look ashamed of himself, a rueful grimace twisting his hard mouth.

'So long as you're all right, Laura,' Tom muttered, moving to the door.

Behind him Randal said quietly, 'I'll make her happy, Nicol, don't worry. You never need to worry about her again. She'll be the most cherished woman in the world.'

Tom stood still, his back to them. After a moment he said, 'Good. Thank you. I'm glad if things have worked out between you.'

Laura wanted to kiss him goodbye, but Randal's jealousy was not dead yet and she knew she could not do it. 'Goodbye, Tom,' she said tenderly. 'Thank you for coming.' The words were meaningless. Her voice said much more without words.

Tom opened the door, closed it and was gone. Randal looked down at her, his face dark with passion. 'I'm sorry I behaved like a crass idiot, but I can't get over the fact that you thought you loved him once.'

Slowly she said, 'I'll always love him.'

Randal's face went wooden. His eyes burnt on her face.

'He was my brother, my friend, almost another father for so many years,' she said as if to herself. 'You can't shut off that sort of affection overnight without doing damage to yourself. Wherever Tom is for the rest of my life I'll miss him.'

'I see,' Randal said quietly, his voice harsh with pain.

She looked at him, shaking her head gently, her eyes tender. 'My dearest, Tom could never come between us again. Don't you know that now? My love for you is deeper, stronger, more passionate than that. Tom is my brother. You ...' She put her arms around his neck and pulled his head down towards her. His mouth closed hungrily over hers as she whispered to him, 'You're my lover.'

Titles available this month in the Mills & Boon ROMANCE Series

LEAF IN THE STORM by *Anne Hampson*
Could the formidable Gavin Huntly help Sally get over the loss of her husband? But all Gavin wanted from their marriage was an heir...

A PLACE FOR LOVERS by *Gwen Westwood*
Debra had problems enough when Vance Spencer set about developing her beloved Cape St. Faith's — she just didn't need to fall in love with him!

THE TAMING OF TAMSIN by *Mary Wibberley*
Tamsin's assignment to look after two small children held no terrors for her — it was Blaise Torran, their uncompromising uncle, who provided all the troubles!

THE DARK SIDE OF MARRIAGE by *Margery Hilton*
Circumstances had forced Nick and Karen Radcliffe together again after two years apart, and although her husband had nothing but contempt for her, Karen still had a desperate longing for him...

PROUD HARVEST by *Anne Mather*
Lesley Radley was determined not to let her small son go to live with his father — but Carne Radley was not going to leave it at that...

THE SAVAGE ARISTOCRAT by *Roberta Leigh*
Kept a virtual prisoner by the autocratic Señor Ramon de la Rivas, Vanessa found herself falling in love with him — but he was already pledged to marry another woman...

THE EMERALD EAGLE by *Jane Corrie*
Sonia was not prepared to let her half-brother use her good looks in his business dealings. She just was *not* interested in the haughty Rory Maragal!

DISTURBING STRANGER by *Charlotte Lamb*
Randal Mercier had made no secret of the fact that he had wanted Laura Hallam from the first moment he saw her — and Randal Mercier usually got what he wanted!

SWEET TORMENT by *Flora Kidd*
Married to, and in love with, Juan Renalda, how could Sorrel be sure that his only reason for marrying her was not to conceal his affair with another woman?

DILEMMA IN PARADISE by *Robyn Donald*
Tamsyn had desperately to fight the attraction between herself and Grant Chapman, because she knew she would never be more than just another in a long line of playthings...

Available September 1978 — Only 50p each

DON'T MISS SEPTEMBER'S GREAT DOCTOR - NURSE ROMANCES

A CALL FOR NURSE TEMPLAR by *Anne Weale*
Young Mrs. Craig, one of Linden's midwifery patients, seemed to be firmly under the thumb of her husband's brother, the arrogant Randal Craig. When Linden found out Randal's opinion of *her*, it was the last straw!

OUTBACK NURSE by *Kerry Mitchell*
The agency's computer said that Jill was ideal to go and work in the bush nursing hospital at Flynn's Creek. But it wasn't programmed to deal with the jealous Sister Furlong's behaviour — nor for Jill to fall in love ...

LOOK OUT FOR THEM AT YOUR NEAREST MILLS & BOON STOCKIST   Only 50p

Also available this month
Four titles in our Mills & Boon Classics Series

Specially chosen re-issues of the best in Romantic Fiction

September's Titles are:

RED FEATHER LOVE
by Suzanna Lynne

When young Gillian McBride went out to Swaziland to live, the first man she met was Dirk von Breda, and the first thing she did was fall hopelessly in love with him. But he had already made his attitude clear: "Precocious kids are not my favourite brand of humanity!"

AN EAGLE SWOOPED
by Anne Hampson

When Paul Demetrius was blinded in an accident and his fiancée Lucinda walked out on him, her sister Tessa, who had always loved Paul, went to him, pretending to be Lucinda. Would her love be strong enough to stand the strain of living such a lie? And what if Paul found out?

MASQUERADE
by Anne Mather

Samantha's famous actress mother was selfishly not prepared to admit to having a twenty-one-year-old daughter, and insisted that she pass herself off as sixteen. But how was it going to affect Samantha's relationship with the handsome and disturbing Patrick Mallory?

HOUSE OF STRANGERS
by Violet Winspear

Marny Lester loved her new job as secretary to an osteopath, and the staff were a friendly crowd. Errol Dennis, in particular, seemed to have taken a liking to her — and it was no good her sighing for Paul Stillman, when he was engaged to the glamorous Ilena Justine.

Mills & Boon Classics

— all that's great in Romantic Reading!

BUY THEM TODAY only 50p

DON'T FORGET TO ASK SANTA FOR YOUR CHRISTMAS PACK
Four favourite authors
First time in paperback

FOUR NEW TITLES
Published October 20th

SCORPIONS' DANCE Anne Mather
AUTUMN CONQUEST Charlotte Lamb
BEWARE OF THE STRANGER Janet Dailey
NIGHT OF LOVE Roberta Leigh
£2.00 net

— CUT-OUT AND POST THIS PAGE TO RECEIVE —

YOUR COPY OF 'HAPPY READING' – THE COMPLETE MILLS & BOON CATALOGUE FREE!

or – if you wish – ORDER NOW from the special selection overleaf!

If you enjoyed this MILLS & BOON romance you'll certainly enjoy choosing *more* of your favourite kind of romantic reading from the exciting, full-colour illustrated pages of 'Happy Reading' — the complete MILLS & BOON Catalogue. 'Happy Reading' lists nearly 400 top-favourite MILLS & BOON Classics and Romances and features details of all our future publications and special offers. It also includes an easy-to-use, DIRECT DELIVERY Order Form which you will find especially useful and convenient if you are having difficulty in obtaining any of the new monthly MILLS & BOON romances from your local stockist.

Just cut-out and post this page *today* — to receive *your* copy of 'Happy Reading' ENTIRELY FREE! Better still: why not order a few of the specially-recommended MILLS & BOON Romances listed over the page *at the same time?* Simply tick your selection(s) overleaf, complete the coupon below, and send the whole page to us with your remittance (including correct postage and packing). All orders despatched by return!

POST TO: MILLS & BOON READER SERVICE: P.O. Box 236, 14 Sanderstead Road, S. Croydon, Surrey CR2 0YG, England.

Please tick ☑(as applicable) below: —

☐ Please send me the FREE Mills & Boon Catalogue
☐ As well as my FREE Catalogue please send me the title(s) I have ticked overleaf

I enclose £_____ (No C.O.D.). Please add 8p. postage and packing per book. *(Maximum Charge: 48p. for 6 or more titles.)*

NAME (Mrs./Miss) _____
ADDRESS _____
CITY/TOWN _____
COUNTY/COUNTRY _____
POSTAL/ZIP CODE _____

*S. African and Rhodesian readers please write to: P.O. Box 11190, Johannesburg 2000, S. Africa.

C1/1429

Choose from this selection of Mills & Boon FAVOURITES
—ALL HIGHLY RECOMMENDED

ORDER NOW FOR DIRECT DELIVERY

- ☐ 1367 THE BRIGHTEST STAR *Roumelia Lane*
- ☐ 1369 CALL BACK YESTERDAY *Charlotte Lamb*
- ☐ 1371 HEART OF THE EAGLE *Elizabeth Graham*
- ☐ 1372 THE AWAKENING OF ALICE *Violet Winspear*
- ☐ 1373 BRITANNIA ALL AT SEA *Betty Neels*
- ☐ 1375 THE ENCHANTED WOODS *Katrina Britt*
- ☐ 1377 LOREN'S BABY *Anne Mather*
- ☐ 1378 IMAGE OF LOVE *Rebecca Stratton*
- ☐ 1379 FOR BITTER OR WORSE *Janet Dailey*
- ☐ 1380 MIDNIGHT MAGIC *Margaret Pargeter*
- ☐ 1381 LOVE FOR A STRANGER *Jane Donnelly*
- ☐ 1382 LORD OF THE ISLAND *Mary Wibberley*
- ☐ 1383 UNDER MOONGLOW *Anne Hampson*
- ☐ 1384 BELOVED SURGEON *Sheila Douglas*
- ☐ 1385 THE GOLDEN GIRL *Elizabeth Ashton*
- ☐ 1386 UNWANTED WIFE *Rachel Lindsay*
- ☐ 1390 THE WILD SWAN *Margaret Way*
- ☐ 1391 THE BROKEN LINK *Yvonne Whittal*
- ☐ 1393 THE DEVIL AT ARCHANGEL *Sara Craven*
- ☐ 1396 THE HILLS OF HOME *Helen Bianchin*

ONLY 50p EACH

SIMPLY TICK ☑ YOUR SELECTION(S) ABOVE, THEN JUST COMPLETE AND POST THE ORDER FORM OVERLEAF ▶